LP - Romance
SD SK
L

GROWING DREAMS

After the death of her long-absent ex-husband, Samantha Rayner and her young daughter Allie move to Pengelly in Cornwall to start afresh. When they stumble across the overgrown grounds of Pengelly Hall, Sam starts dreaming of restoring them to their former glory. Jackson Clark, the business-minded owner of Pengelly Hall, agrees to fund the project, but could Sam have taken on more than she bargained for . . . And what secrets does head gardener Will Heston hold in his past?

CHRISSIE LOVEDAY

GROWING DREAMS

Complete and Unabridged

LINFORD
Leicester

First published in Great Britain in 2006

First Linford Edition
published 2006

British Library CIP Data

Loveday, Chrissie
    Growing dreams.—Large print ed.—
Linford romance library
    1. Gardens—Conservation and restoration—
Fiction
    2. Cornwall (England)—Fiction
    3. Love stories 4. Large type books
    I. Title
    823.9'14 [F]

ISBN 1–84617–530–5

Published by
F. A. Thorpe (Publishing)
Anstey, Leicestershire
Set by Words & Graphics Ltd.
Anstey, Leicestershire
Printed and bound in Great Britain by
T. J. International Ltd., Padstow, Cornwall

This book is printed on acid-free paper

A Fresh Start

When she read the advert in the paper, Samantha Rayner closed her eyes. Pengelly. She thought of sunny holidays with her parents; buckets and spades and rock pools. She and Phil, her younger brother, had spent their holiday lives building dams to stop the tide from washing away their ephemeral treasures. Pengelly.

It was a lifetime ago. Everything had changed since those far-off days. Could they possibly go there, to live?

She thought about it for hours. Dare she risk it? Should she gamble everything on what was little more than a whim? Wouldn't hurt to phone. Find out a few more details. She frowned. From now on, she had to watch the cost of every call she made.

She read the advert again: *Small cottage available in return for light shop*

duties and help with housework.
Cornish village of Pengelly. Quiet
location. Suit single person. Apply Mrs
Lucinda Johns.

Sam wondered if it could be *their*
Mrs Johns? But no, surely that wasn't
possible. She had been an old lady even
then. Maybe she was a daughter, or
perhaps Lucinda could be her son's
wife.

With shaking fingers, she dialled the
number. Single person? What about
Allie?

★　★　★

That had been the start of her new life.
Hers and Allie's. Her nine-year-old
daughter had been thrilled by the
prospect of living next to the sea . . . at
first. But then, as she had watched the
only home she had ever known
disappearing into boxes, the full realisa-
tion had hit the child.

Those few days had been a night-
mare. Allie had sulked, cried, tried

every trick, including being physically sick, to make her mother change her mind about the move. In desperation, Sam had finally called her brother, Phil, over, hoping he could reassure the little girl that Pengelly was truly the beautiful place she remembered.

After a long walk with her uncle, Allie had returned red-eyed and quiet, and sullenly set about packing her things, apparently reconciled to the idea. If they really did have to leave their home, it might as well be to somewhere quite new. The friends and familiar surroundings would be too far away to return.

Sam knew that a complete redirection of their lives was long overdue.

'Are we really poor now, Mummy?' Allie had asked. It was obviously something that had begun to infiltrate her mind, following her talk with Phil.

'I'm afraid so, darling. This house had to be sold and now we have to leave it very quickly.'

Sam had had to steel herself against the ridiculous urge to cry. The recent news of Martin's death had come as a tremendous shock. He had died in a plane crash, identified only by some luggage and a passport that had somehow been recovered, but she hadn't shed a single tear at the time. Although he had walked out on her and their small daughter eight years ago, she had been lulled into a sort of numbness.

He had dutifully paid the mortgage on their modest house through the years, while the small but regular allowance for Allie had meant they could live comfortably enough as long as she was careful. Their lives had ticked on, making ends meet, helped by Sam's occasional part-time jobs.

Now, all of that was ended. She had lived with a peculiar sense of security over the years, assuming things would continue this way for ever. When Martin had died, so had her scant security. Even selling the house had barely covered the amount outstanding on the mortgage.

Martin. Sam could scarcely even remember what he had looked like, even less that she had once loved him so passionately. When the solicitor's letter had arrived, she had shed no tears for her ex-husband, but now, weeks later, every few moments his memory crept back, along with regrets that she had buried long ago.

Yes, it was high time she made the move, even if it tore her away from every last vestige of the man she had known and loved.

'It's sad that my daddy has died,' Allie said, in quite a matter-of-fact tone. 'I won't ever get to see him now. Are we taking my bedroom curtains?' she added in the same breath, showing precisely how very remote Martin must have seemed to her.

Sam put a hand on her shoulder. 'You'll love Cornwall,' she promised, crossing her fingers as she spoke. 'I'm sure it'll be extra beautiful in the spring.'

Whatever she herself felt about

leaving her home, *their* home, it brought a sense of finality. That part of her life was well and truly over.

★ ★ ★

Two weeks later, as she glanced round the tiny cottage, she bit her lip as the doubts set in. She had given the one decent-sized bedroom to Allie. Her own room was little more than a large shelf above one side of the sitting-room. Once a single bed was in place there was no room for anything else. Her clothes would have to stay in the airing cupboard and in a chest of drawers in the bathroom. Allie needed space of her own, somewhere to put her treasures, and in a couple of years she would have homework, when her own room would be essential. It was the only solution.

Lucinda Johns, the original, had given them a rapturous welcome. To Sam she looked very much as she remembered. Obviously, it had been the usual case of anyone over thirty looking old to a child! Lucinda even claimed that she could remember Sam and her brother.

'Your little girl is the very spit of you at that age.' She smiled fondly. 'Same blonde hair, even the same little pony-tail. I just hope you'll manage in that tiny place. I never really expected anyone with a child to live there.'

'We'll be fine,' Sam assured the kindly woman, though she had her doubts. It would be a great strain on both of them after their comparatively spacious home in Hertfordshire. But mother and daughter were good friends, driven together by their mutual needs.

Lucinda arranged the hours that Sam would be working in the shop, trying to make them coincide with Allie's school times. The housework part of the deal could be done at weekends, when Allie could accompany her and Lucinda was in the shop. It all seemed quite straightforward. The house and a small wage would allow them to survive, at least for the foreseeable future. Who could ever begin to guess at what might lie ahead?

'We should make the most of the rest of your holiday,' Sam said brightly, after two days spent unpacking. 'What would you like to do?'

'Go to the beach,' Allie said firmly.

While they pottered around the rock pools, Sam told Allie about the things she and her brother, Phil, had done on childhood holidays, damming streams, making lakes and miniature waterfalls, just as children have always done.

They wandered along the beach to the high rocky cliffs at the sides.

'I bet Uncle Phil always wanted to climb up here,' Allie said.

Sam nodded, the years and memories rolling along together like some great pile of tumbleweed.

'The beach looked different each year. It's the way beaches are, I suppose. The holiday-makers only see them during their own holidays and think they always look like that.'

'Well, I'm glad we aren't just

holiday-makers. We can see exactly what the beach looks like all year round now, can't we?'

'We certainly can, love. Shall we go up the path and see the view from the top?'

Allie nodded and they climbed the steep cliff path. At the top, they looked over the wooded valleys and sparkling blue sea.

'Neat place,' Allie commented, much to her mother's relief. Fingers crossed, it might just work, she thought.

They wandered farther along the cliff top, towards the thick tangle of trees, neglected and overgrown, stretching away inland.

'It's like a magic forest,' Allie said, her eyes wide. 'There could be witches and goblins in a forest like that. Hobbits too, I expect.'

Sam smiled, gazing around with interest. 'There are some quite unusual trees here. Unusual for Cornwall. I think this whole forest must have been specially planted at some time. These trees certainly aren't native to this part of the world.'

'You've been reading Grandpa's books again, haven't you?'

'Not really. I was always interested in helping him when he had his own nursery garden.'

They walked along silently for a while, Sam peering closely at the many different trees. She was intrigued to find out the history of this valley.

'I'm hungry,' Allie announced. Further exploration of the forest would have to wait.

* * *

While her daughter was battling with a new school, Sam quickly established her routine of working in the shop each morning, and whenever she was free she wandered through the strange wooded valley nearby.

After refreshing her memory from her father's old books, she could put names to many of the species of trees, a large number of them from distant parts of the world. Once, many years earlier, someone had planted this wood with love and care and an eye for the unusual.

She glanced at her watch. She had just over an hour before Allie came home and she was determined to find out what lay beyond the wood. She clambered up a steep slope, slipping in the damp mud left by a stream that cascaded down. She pushed her way through a tangle of bushes and reached an open space. Coarse grassland dotted with yellow buttercups stretched out before her.

'This is private property. You're trespassing,' came a loud voice.

She looked up and saw a man standing watching her.

'I'm sorry. I was interested to see what's at the edge of the wood,' she said, breathless from her climb.

'Wood's private too,' said the man, sounding grumpy. He was scruffily dressed and well-tanned, as if he worked outdoors most of the time. His body was lean and his hands were working hands.

'I'm sorry. I didn't see any signs. I was intrigued by the wide variety of trees. Someone took great trouble to cultivate this valley. Is there a house nearby?'

'There *was* a house here. Only now it's being turned into apartments. Criminal if you ask me. But his lordship decided that's the way to go. Made himself a tidy fortune out of it as well, I don't doubt. Not even as if he needed the money,' he added sourly.

'Oh, and who is 'his lordship'?' she asked.

'I'm not sure I should divulge that sort of information to a trespasser. He likes his privacy.'

Sam stared. Had she imagined the twinkle in his eyes? He sounded fierce enough, but maybe he was teasing her? She coloured slightly.

'Jackson Clark,' he announced.

'I beg your pardon? Oh, the owner?'

Sam replied. 'So what? Who's he?'

'You must have heard of him. Something to do with computers. Very important man, so they say.'

'Oh, computers. I have nothing to do with those wretched things!' She smiled and watched carefully for any sign of relaxation in the forbidding expression on his face. 'I'm Samantha Rayner — Sam. I've just moved down here to Mrs Johns' cottage in the village.'

'Will Heston,' he returned. 'I'm in charge of the grounds here. Though exactly what anyone expects one man can do in a massive place like this is beyond me. By the time the lawns are cut and a few of the beds tidied, that's it. But Mr Jackson Clark's simply not interested. When he's here, he spends all his days indoors — thumping away at his computer, I guess. Only time he showed any interest was when the architect drew up the plans for the conversion. I expect he was working out how much he was likely to make out of the deal.' He sounded very bitter about his employer.

'Look, I'd love to know more about this place but I have to go now,' Sam said, hesitating. She very much wanted to continue this conversation, but Allie would be home soon. 'Is there anyone I could talk to? Your Mr Jackson, for instance?'

'Mr Clark. His name's Jackson Clark. But I doubt if you'll ever see him. He's always flying off round the world.'

'I gather you don't much like him,' Sam remarked.

He gave a non-committal shrug, then added, 'I'd be pleased to show you round the garden, such as it is, if you really are interested.'

'Thanks, that would be great. My next afternoon off is Friday but I have to be back for my daughter soon after four.'

He smiled, his teeth very white against the tanned face. He was really quite good-looking, she thought, and the thought surprised her. It was a very long time since she had been conscious of any man's looks.

'I'll meet you here about two then,' Will offered. 'You know something about gardening?'

'What makes you say that?'

'You must be the first person to notice the trees, let alone know that they're not native.'

'My father had a specialist nursery when I was a kid. I suppose my interest began there. Look, I must go. I'll see you on Friday. Thanks. Bye!'

As she walked back through the wood, she felt her heart beating a little faster. She had the feeling that she was on the edge of something new. Quite ridiculous. She couldn't possibly have been attracted to this gardener, could she? She was far too old for such thoughts! A single mother with a daughter to support? For heaven's sake, she was over thirty!

She supposed she wasn't too bad for her age. Her honey-coloured hair was thick and naturally wavy and she had always managed to keep herself fit, even if she had always considered herself to be too tall to be attractive. Most men made her feel ungainly. Except for Martin. He had been a big man and she had always been comfortable with him.

But then, she had only to remind herself of what had happened after the early years. At the time, she had convinced herself that if she and a one-year-old baby could be deserted by her husband, she obviously wasn't in the least attractive.

She frowned. She had only been in Pengelly for a couple of weeks or so. What on earth was she doing even thinking about such things? She had never once, in the lonely years, considered allowing another man into her life. Now, just because some gardener had stopped to chat to her, she was behaving totally out of character. It was ridiculous.

But deep inside, she knew her feelings of something new impending were much more than simply meeting the man. Something momentous was surely waiting around the corner.

★ ★ ★

'Where were you, Mummy?' Allie demanded from the doorstep when her mother rushed through the gate of their tiny cottage.

'I went for a walk and it took me longer to get back than I expected. Have you been home long?'

'Hours,' Allie said dramatically. 'I couldn't get in. I didn't know what to do. Where to go or anything. And I'm starving.'

They went inside and soon Sam had the kettle on and the tin of biscuits at hand. They chatted companionably, recounting the trivial details of their day as they always did. Oddly, Sam mentioned neither Will Heston nor their arrangement to meet again. She tried to tell herself that it was simply because it was unimportant. After all, she knew nothing at all about him except that he was a gardener.

★ ★ ★

She was surprised to realise that she felt quite nervous by the time Friday afternoon arrived. Will was leaning against a tree when she arrived hot and rather dishevelled.

'Hi,' he said. 'I wondered if you'd come or whether you might have changed your mind.'

'Why would I do that? I'm very interested in the whole place. It's good of you to spare the time to show me round.'

He gave her a friendly grin and heaved his large frame upright.

They walked towards the house, a once magnificent country home, probably around a hundred and fifty years old. It was in a sorry state at present, with the mess and debris of building work littering the place. Many of the original windows had been removed while the work was being done, and the whole place had a rather desolate air, as if it didn't quite understand this transition.

'I suppose it'll all get straight again one day,' Will grumbled. 'Luxury apartments seem a mighty long way off at present. They've made a terrible mess of my flower borders but I s'pose they'll recover.'

'It must have been quite some place in its heyday,' Sam remarked. 'Must have cost a fortune to keep up. Why do you think Mr Clark bought it?'

'The original family had all gone. Line had evidently died out. It was put up for sale and stood empty for years and years. Clark bought it a couple of years ago. He's kept one apartment for his own use. That's been left pretty much as it was, I believe. There's a housekeeper lives in and she looks after his living quarters. Funny old life though, it seems to me. You'd think someone who'd bought all this would at least want to live here, wouldn't you?'

'Too much space for one, perhaps? Bit different from me! We've hardly got room to swing a cat. Not that we've got one — a cat, I mean. Allie takes up far more room than any cat, but we'll manage.'

'And what of Mr Rayner?'

She stared at him for a moment, then suddenly found herself blurting out her life story as they wandered round the garden.

After several minutes, she paused and stood still. 'I'm so sorry,' she mumbled in embarrassment. 'I don't know what came over me, rabbiting on like that. I never talk about Martin, not to anyone.'

Will smiled, showing even white teeth. 'Maybe the time was right. You needed to break a few silences. I've been told I'm a good listener.'

'But what about you? You haven't told me anything about yourself.'

He shrugged. 'Nothing very interesting to tell. I was born near here, lived here most of my life and now I work here. That's about it.' He plainly wasn't going to volunteer much more and Sam was reluctant to appear too curious.

She turned to indicate a dilapidated

wall that might once have surrounded a kitchen garden.

'You don't attempt to grow any vegetables, I take it?' she asked.

'No point. There's no-one to eat them. I grow some for myself in my own garden, of course. Besides, like I said, keeping a few decent flower-beds near the house is about the best I can do with the time I have. The lawns are usually kept cut but I've even given up the fight against the diggers for the moment. Maybe when the apartments are sold, someone may take an interest and want to do a bit more.'

'But why was it all abandoned this way? It's as if everyone left and the place simply went to sleep, like Sleeping Beauty's castle.'

'I think that's just what did happen. The local story goes that the men had to leave the country to go to fight in the First World War. After that, the few who did return no longer wanted to work in a place like this. The old family had all but died off. When the last owner died, she was a spinster, and there was no-one connected with the family to carry it on. The proceeds of the sale went to some remote relative.'

'How very sad,' Sam said, an unexpected lump in her throat.

Once they had reached the end of the lawn, the garden retreated into wild tangles of bushes and shrubs. A few daffodils were still blooming, almost lost among the rough grass and weeds.

Sam half-closed her eyes, imagining what it must have been like with the vast stretches of lawn and colourful banks of flowers everywhere. In reality, she could see huge tangles of rhododendron bushes, azaleas, camellias and many more species she didn't recognise. They were all here, though neglected and overgrown; they seemed to be awaiting someone's love and care to bring them back to full life. Only a few patches of colour showed where the blossoms managed to survive.

'Sleeping beauties themselves,' she

whispered and he gave her another of his rare smiles.

'You're quite a romantic at heart, aren't you?' he said.

She tensed, her lips drawing into a hard line. What was she doing, allowing anyone even a glimpse into her mind?

'I've no time or space for silly romantic thoughts,' she said briskly, and glanced at her watch. 'I must hurry. I can't have Allie getting home to an empty house. She was practically on the verge of calling the police when I was a bit late the other day.'

'I'll drive you back round the road way. It'll be quicker. If you don't mind my ancient Land-Rover, that is,' Will offered.

Uncertain, Sam glanced at her watch again. It took more than twenty minutes to walk back through the wood and it was already quarter to four.

'I don't want to bother you.'

'Wouldn't offer if it was any bother. Mr Clark's away so he'll never know what time I left. Not that I'm worried about hours. I work more than my fair share, considering. Come on — it's parked just round the back here.' He gave a shrill whistle and a Jack Russell came streaking out of the undergrowth.

'Is he yours? He's a sweetie. No, get down boy. You're all muddy,' she protested, laughing.

'She — Jenny. You've been digging again, you wretched dog, haven't you? The building work seems to have uncovered ancient rat trails going back through centuries. Get in the back, girl. Would you believe that's supposed to be a *white* dog?'

Sam laughed, petting the lively little animal. 'If you don't like mud, don't get a dog! I'd forgotten what fun dogs can be.'

'No good having a dog if you're prone to cat-swinging, though,' Will remarked as he drove down the heavily-furrowed drive. 'Wretched builders. I doubt this place will ever recover,' he said, scowling. 'Now, where in the village do you live?'

A few minutes later, they stopped

outside the cottage. She hesitated, wondering about asking him in for a cup of tea. It seemed only polite, but she was doubtful about Allie's reaction to finding a strange man in her home. The few minutes after school were always their own special time.

She took a deep breath to calm nerves that were suddenly jangling.

'Would you like a cup of tea?' she asked.

'Thought you'd never ask,' he replied. 'I'd love one.' He leapt out of the ancient vehicle and went round to open Sam's door.

The little dog rushed forward in excitement.

'Get back, Jen. You shouldn't risk coming into this house. Apart from the mud, they might swing you round by the tail! In the absence of a cat, that is.'

They walked up the little path and Sam unlocked the door. She put the kettle on as Will stood in the doorway of the tiny kitchen, watching her.

'Compact isn't the word,' Sam said

with a laugh. 'But we manage. Allie will be back soon,' she added. Will was a large man, making the tiny room seem even smaller. 'Do sit down,' she urged, looking anxiously through the window for Allie. She didn't want her to be upset at finding a stranger in her home.

The kettle turned itself off and she was warming the tea-pot when the door burst open and Allie hurtled into the room. 'I'm home, Mum,' she yelled and stopped. 'Oh,' was her only comment.

'Allie, this is Mr Heston. He's the gardener who works near that wood we found.'

'Will. Call me Will,' he said, holding out his hand. 'I'm pleased to meet you, Allie.'

She hesitated then, uncertainly, held out her own little hand. She smiled and turned to her mother. 'I'm starving, is there anything to eat?' she asked.

Sam laughed. Some things never changed.

'I'd Like To See You Again . . .'

Will seemed relaxed and chatted with Allie about school and her new life in Cornwall while Sam listened, realising how few men her daughter had talked to in her life. She was too young to remember her father, and apart from Sam's brother Phil she had spent very little time in male company.

Will was understanding and seemed able to relate to Allie very comfortably. In fact, he looked totally at ease, sitting in her tiny living-room.

'Look, I've had an idea,' Will said suddenly. 'Why don't we all go out somewhere? We could go to one of the local theme parks. I don't suppose you've had much time to get out and about since you arrived.'

'I'm not sure,' Sam said quickly.

'We're broke,' Allie announced, much to her mother's annoyance.

'Allie,' she snapped. 'Don't say such things.'

'You said we couldn't afford to go anywhere any more. You even sold the car before we moved down here,' Allie elaborated bluntly.

'I know, but Mr Heston doesn't want to know about our private affairs.'

'Don't worry,' he said reassuringly, 'I understand. But I was inviting you to be my guests, of course. Think about it, and if you would do me the honour of accompanying me, let me know.'

'We will. We do. Thank you, Will. We'd like go, wouldn't we, Mum?' Allie was quite positive.

'I'm really not sure it's a good idea . . . ' Sam began.

'I'd be glad of your company,' Will interrupted.

'Come on, Mummy. Say we can go. Please?'

'Oh, all right then.' She gave a half-hearted smile. 'Thanks, Will. It's a kind thought.'

He looked pleased and grinned

broadly at them both. 'I'll be the envy of everyone, with two lovely ladies beside me,' he said.

They sat for a while longer, drinking tea, Allie chatting nineteen to the dozen, all about her new school and the children in her class.

Will seemed to be listening intently and Sam took the opportunity to study him. He must be a similar age to herself. He had startlingly blue eyes and his mid-brown hair was bleached at the tips where it was exposed to the sun. He had a rugged appeal, not conventionally good-looking but pleasant enough. His clothes were practical, far removed from anything that could be called stylish. The jeans had certainly seen better days and his sweater was baggy and comfortable looking.

He was just about the exact opposite of her ex-husband, Martin. *Late* husband Martin, she mentally corrected, feeling an unexpected pang. When he had gone off to live in Australia, it had made him seem remote and she had tried to push away all thoughts of him. The finality of his death must have roused some long-forgotten memories.

'Can we go this Sunday, Mummy? Please say yes,' Allie was burbling.

'I'm sorry, I was miles away. What did you say?' Sam blushed slightly, embarrassed at her daydreaming.

'Can we go with Will on Sunday? To Flambards?' Allie pressed.

'Well, I'm not really sure. It's rather expensive . . .'

'As I said, my treat. I insist. I'll pick you up around ten. That'll give us plenty of time to get there for opening time. I'm afraid the Land-Rover's a bit bumpy but it usually gets there.'

Sam was troubled. Her independence was in danger of being compromised, but it didn't seem fair to deprive Allie of a treat. Heaven knew, there would be little chance for treats in the foreseeable future.

'I'll pack us a picnic,' Sam offered. 'It can be my contribution to the day.'

'Sounds great,' Will said. 'Right, now

that's all decided, I'd better get home.'

'Where do you live?' Allie asked.

'In the lodge at Pengelly Hall. Goes with the job. You'll have to bring your mum to see it one day. I can make you some tea, to thank you for today.'

He left and Sam and Allie went to the garden gate to see him off. Jenny was bouncing around in the Land-Rover, barking her welcome and the end to her wait.

'You've got a dog!' Allie cried in excitement. 'Why didn't you bring him in? He's lovely. Hello, boy!' she said as she put her hands against the window. Jenny leapt around in even greater excitement.

'She's a girl dog and her name's Jenny. She's a naughty little dog, always going down rabbit holes and coming back covered in mud. Not fit for any civilised home, I'm afraid.' Will smiled at the child's enthusiasm and was about to say something else but then changed his mind. It was obviously not appropriate at this time. With a wave, he

31

climbed into the vehicle and rattled off down the road.

'He's nice,' Allie announced. 'I hope he sticks around for a while. Thank heavens it's Friday. I'm all burned out. Bushed.' She bounced off back inside the cottage.

Sam laughed. Where did Allie pick up such phrases? It came to something when a nine-year-old claimed to be suffering from stress!

* * *

It was dull on Sunday morning and Sam added rain gear to her rucksack along with the picnic. Allie was full of high spirits at the thought of a day out and chattered excitedly about the wonders she was about to experience at the theme park. Sam tried her best not to deflate her in any way but she herself was far less confident about the day ahead. After all, she hardly knew Will. Two brief meetings and a shared cup of tea and here she was, about to spend a whole day with him! She tried to tell herself it was all for Allie and that she would never even have considered spending time with him on her own.

'He's here, Mummy,' yelled Allie. She had been looking out for him since soon after nine. 'I think he may have Jenny with him. I hope so.' She rushed to open the door and bounded up the path. 'Hi, Will. We're all ready. Have you brought Jenny?'

'Good morning, Allie. How are you? Jenny's in the Land-Rover, so I hope you aren't too bothered by dog hairs. You'll have to sit in the back with her.'

'Aw, neat,' Allie replied. 'One of the girls at school told me there's this brilliant ride. Practically turns you upside down and whizzes around all the corners. You'd better go on that *before* lunch, Mum, or you'll probably be sick.'

'I'll possibly give that one a miss, thank you very much,' Sam protested.

'You can't!' Allie squealed. 'Kids aren't allowed to go on their own and I want to go on that most of all.'

'I may have to risk my own life and limb then,' Will said with a laugh. 'Gosh, I'm looking forward to today. I haven't been on any of those sorts of rides for years.'

'Don't worry, I'll look after you,' Allie assured him.

Sam almost envied the little girl's lack of self-consciousness and the ease with which she had taken to this comparative stranger. Undoubtedly, the little dog helped to break the ice. Allie had been pestering to have a dog for years but it had never seemed the right time. Now, in this tiny cottage, it was quite out of the question.

'Isn't Jenny the most beautiful dog you've ever seen?' Allie inquired. 'Her lovely little chubby body and such a sweet face. I like the black bit on her back. It's like a little saddle. Come on, girl, wag your tail.' She prattled on happily, obviously in her seventh heaven.

'You OK?' asked Will, noticing Sam's own silence.

'Fine,' she replied. 'I just know when I'm beaten. Trying to get a word in is impossible when she's in this mood!'

He smiled at her, his eyes crinkling at the corners, and she realised with surprise that he was very comfortable to be with. She relaxed and began to enjoy the day. Will might prove to be a good friend to them as long as everything was kept simple and uncomplicated.

The rain held off and the trio managed to go on every ride, visit every display and ate every last bit of the picnic.

'I meant to save something for Jenny,' wailed Allie. 'But I got so hungry, I ate everything. Poor little Jenny, left in the car.'

'She'll be fine,' Will assured her. 'She has plenty of fresh air and it isn't sunny, so she won't be too hot. You have to be careful about leaving dogs in cars so she only comes with me if I know it isn't going to be sunny. And don't worry about food. She's quite fat enough without being stuffed with titbits! And she loves being in the car. Now, anyone for ice cream?'

They sat in a row on the wall, legs swinging as they licked their ices. To passers-by, they must have looked like any ordinary family out for the day. But Sam was conscious that Will wasn't a part of their little family and suddenly felt a pang of anxiety. If Allie got too used to having him around, it would come as a shock when he disappeared again.

Undoubtedly Will was very good with her daughter, and she wondered if he'd been married himself, maybe had children of his own. Or perhaps he'd had younger siblings and that was what made him so much at ease with the little girl.

'I don't know about anyone else, but I think it's time we were leaving,' Sam said a few minutes later. 'It'll be seven by the time we get home and you have school in the morning, Allie.'

The usual protests ensued but gently Will steered them towards the exit.

Jenny was ecstatic when she saw them again. She was let out in the car park and rushed around madly for a few minutes until she was happy to jump back inside the Land-Rover and gave Allie a thorough licking as they drove home.

'Can Will stay for supper?' she asked when they arrived back at the cottage.

'Well, I was only going to do something quick. But, of course, if you'd like to stay?' Sam said uncertainly.

'Thanks, but I think I'd better get back home and give Jenny her supper. We've had a long day out and I'm sure you're both tired. Another time though, perhaps?'

Allie moaned a little but caught her mother's warning glance. She knew better than to make a fuss.

'Of course,' Sam replied gratefully. She needed a bit of time to herself to try to come to terms with her innermost thoughts. They thanked him and climbed out of the Land-Rover.

'Come and visit the garden whenever you feel like it,' Will offered. 'I'm usually around, but in any case, I'm sure no-one will mind.'

'Thanks, I may well do that. Thank you again. It's been a lovely day.'

They waved as he drove away, Jenny's little face peeping out of the back and her tail wagging as they drove out of sight.

'Isn't he nice, Mummy?' Allie said as she was tucked up in bed. Sam nodded and kissed her goodnight.

She went downstairs and sat down in front of the television. But her thoughts weren't on the programme. She felt confused at seeing a man looking as if he was a part of her family. She wondered why he was paying them such attention. As long as he was simply being kind, that was fine, but if he had any further expectations, she was less certain. But there was Allie to consider. She seemed very taken with Will — or maybe it was Jenny that was the big attraction.

Sam worried for her daughter. Forced to grow up without knowing a father, she could get too attached to Will.

Trying to be objective, she tried to see herself closer to him. He was very nice, seemed reliable and was a good companion. But although it was very early days, she had a feeling friendship was probably the most she could expect from him. She hoped Allie would understand.

★　★　★

As the evenings drew out, Sam and Allie got into the habit of taking a walk after supper. Sometimes they took the cliff path and went towards the Pengelly woods. Pink thrift covered all the walls and hung over the cliffs in huge cushions. The white flowers of the wild garlic gave a pungent perfume to the air.

At other times, they pottered along the beach, picking up shells and seaweed. The repetitive sound of the waves breaking on the shore had a timeless quality. Sam found herself transported back to her childhood. Why had they never found the forest in those days? It must have been there. Her father would have loved it. She shook herself. She was becoming obsessed with the place.

'Come on, love,' she called. 'It's time we were getting back.'

'I'm very glad we came here to live,' Allie confided. 'Even if they don't have many good shops here, it's a very nice place to be, isn't it?

'I think so. I'm pleased that you think we did the right thing.'

Companionably, the two walked back to the little cottage. The beautiful scenery seemed therapeutic and Sam felt more relaxed than for many years.

Once Allie was in bed, she pulled out her father's old books about plants.

She had few reminders of her parents. There was a small collection of jewellery, none of it worth much except in sentimental value, and her father's books. Her parents had died within a few months of each other. Five, no, it must be six years ago. How time flies, she thought with a shock.

Those years had held some desperate moments for Sam. She had felt very alone and knew that her brother Phil was the one who had helped her through it. They had grown closer during those awful months and she valued her brother and sister-in-law as good friends though they were rather a long way away now that she'd brought herself to Cornwall.

'Snap out of it,' she told herself.

She pulled out some sheets of paper and began to make a list of various trees and shrubs she remembered from her last visit. Excitedly she identified them in her books and couldn't wait to visit the valley garden again. Maybe she and Allie could take a picnic early one evening. Meantime, she would ask anyone she could about the history of the mysterious garden.

Mrs Johns remembered little of the family who had once lived there. She had been a child when the house was declining. Some of the women from the village had been maids there and her own grandfather had been one of the gardeners.

'But it's all too long ago for me to remember properly,' she said. 'I used to know Emily Roberts quite well. Years ago, before she was married. She might be able to help. Or you could try the local library, p'raps,' she suggested.

Sam made a trip into the local town at the next opportunity but there was scant information available at the library. The only reference she could find was of the Westcott family home which had been built on the site of an ancient monastery some hundred and fifty years ago.

That evening, she and Allie took pasties with them and walked up through the wood. When they reached the edge of the wood Allie had her first glimpse of the house.

'It's sad, isn't it? Poor house. No-one cares any more,' she said.

'It's being turned into apartments so there will be heaps of people to care about it.'

'Yes, but the man who owns it must be a bit peculiar to have such a lovely house and then to ruin it.' The childish logic was indisputable.

'Maybe he won't ruin it. It could be very nice when it's finished,' Sam suggested.

'Where does Will work? Do you think we'll see him? P'raps Jenny would like to come for a walk?' Allie said hopefully.

'I expect he's finished work for the day. He's probably at home, getting his supper. Shall we sit here and eat our pasties?' Sam asked.

They sat amongst the bushes at the edge of the garden and munched their tasty meal until a scuffling in the bushes made them both jump. A small white dog leapt on them, tail wagging and excited yaps.

'Jenny!' yelled Allie. 'Good dog, come here.'

'Now who have I found trespassing today?' said Will, in a fierce-sounding voice.

'You said we could come when we wanted,' Allie said, looking marginally scared.

'Well, if it isn't my favourite ladies,' he said with a broad grin.

Sam looked up at him, slightly embarrassed by the warmth of his greeting. She hauled herself up and smiled at him rather shyly. 'We came for another little snoop. I tried to find some books in the library about the place but there was hardly anything.'

'Then I shall introduce you to Mrs Roberts. She's the housekeeper here. She might let you have a look at the old library, what's left of it. I think most of the books have been packed up now but there may be something around. Why are you so interested in such a decaying pile of old junk?'

'I'm not sure. I feel there is some story here, waiting to be discovered. Somebody cared very much indeed at one time. It's got to me. Why was it abandoned? This was once such a cherished place. The variety of plants is quite extraordinary, you must know that.'

'You're lovely when you're enthusiastic,' Will remarked, as if he hadn't been listening to a word she'd said.

She blushed, looking round to see if Allie had heard his comments.

'It's all right,' he assured her, 'Allie's busy bonding with Jenny. Look, I'd really like to see you again. Will you come out for a drink sometime?'

'I can't. There's Allie. I mean, I couldn't leave her,' she said evasively.

'You could get a babysitter. I'm sure there's someone you could ask.'

Sam wasn't sure that she wanted to spend too much time alone with him. He might start getting ideas she wouldn't be able to handle.

'I hardly know anyone. Besides, I'm not sure it's a good idea. We don't know each other,' she added feebly.

'Isn't that the whole point? If we don't spend time together, how do we get to know each other? I'd like to spend some time with you. What's wrong with that?'

'Maybe you could come for supper one evening,' she suggested in desperation.

'That would be nice. But I'd like to spend time with you on your own. Allie's a really great kid but I'd like to get to know you as well.'

Sam sighed. It was all so difficult. She didn't want to hurt his feelings but Will Heston was really not her sort of man. In fact, she doubted she could ever dare care about any man again.

She looked at his kindly face. Not the sort of looks she usually went for at all. But what did looks matter? It was the person, the inner being, that was important. And Will was kind and wonderful with her daughter.

Anyway, maybe she was reading much more into his suggestions than he was intending.

'I'm not sure I'm really ready for this,' she said feebly.

Will's face darkened. 'I'm asking you out for a drink, for goodness' sake, not a lifelong commitment! Look, forget it. I'd better be going anyway.'

'Wait, Will. I'm sorry. All I meant was . . . Oh, I don't know what I meant! Look, I'd love to have a drink with you. You're quite right. We do need to get to know each other better. Especially if we might . . . ' She paused and bit her lip. She had been about to say 'work together', but that was jumping more than several guns. Subconsciously she had been fantasising about plans for restoring the old gardens at Pengelly Hall. But that was no more than a dream and a very long way off in the future.

'If we might what?' he asked, looking puzzled.

She smiled. 'I was going to say, if we

might have to cope with a little dog and a little girl who adore each other,' she lied quickly, seeing Allie coming through the bushes with a wriggling Jenny clutched in her arms.

'Jenny wants something to eat. Can I give her some of the pasty leftovers?' she called.

Sam smiled. 'And exactly what leftovers were you thinking of? There isn't even a crumb left.'

'It's time I went home and gave her a proper supper then, don't you think?' Will said quickly.

Reluctantly Allie handed the dog over. 'When can I see her again?' she demanded.

'Soon,' promised Will, his gaze fixed on Sam's face. 'I'll give you a call.'

'But we haven't got a phone,' wailed Allie. She wasn't prepared to leave it to some chance encounter. She wanted a firm date all arranged before they parted.

Will pulled a scrap of paper out of his pocket and scribbled his own number, then handed it to Allie.

'There, now you have Jenny's number and you can call her whenever you like. I always leave the answering machine on, so if I'm not there, you can leave a message for her. I'll wait to hear from you.'

Clearly the message was meant for Sam. He was firmly placing the ball in her court. Whatever the next move was to be, it would come from her.

'Thanks, Will,' she called quickly.

'Yes, thanks, Will. Bye, Jenny,' Allie joined in. She giggled. 'He made it sound as if Jenny could answer the phone all by herself. He's nice,' she added decisively.

'Yes,' agreed Sam. 'He is.'

A Voyage Of Discovery

For the next few days, Sam spent every spare moment poring over her father's old books. She made notes on trees, shrubs and plants of all kinds, realising that she had stumbled on a place that had once been cultivated without any thought of expense.

She could visualise a parkland of great beauty. The valley itself was a natural miracle, hidden in a deep cleft between the cliffs. The micro-climate allowed even sub-tropical plants and trees to flourish. The siting of the actual house had been chosen with great skill, to provide what must be one of the most beautiful views in Cornwall . . . possibly in Britain, she mused.

Allie kept staring at her mother as the days passed. She had never seen her behave like this before. Sam had always been an outdoors person, liking long walks and gardening; she had never spent hours reading this way.

'What on earth are you doing, Mummy?' she asked repeatedly.

'Playing at detectives,' Sam said.

'Can I play as well?' Allie asked.

'Of course. There's a lot of work ahead.'

Allie flopped down on the floor beside Sam's chair, listening intently.

'The first thing I want to do is to identify as many of the trees as we can. I'm making a list, using Grandpa's books to check them out.'

'But there's hundreds and hundreds of trees! It'll take forever.'

'Not really. There's heaps of things growing there that are just weeds and rubbish. I only want to find the really unusual ones.'

Gradually Allie began to share some of her mother's enthusiasm and they made plans to go to the valley the next weekend. In the meantime, Sam planned to visit Pengelly Hall and try to persuade the housekeeper to let her see the library. Perhaps there would be some old records there, even pictures to give clues about the gardens as they once were.

She felt a strange mixture of excitement and trepidation as she stood outside the heavy oak door of the hall the next day. The contractors were working further along the building and had made their own entrance.

At last she heard movements behind the door and a small, grey-haired woman looked out. She wore a floral overall completely covering her clothes, while her sparse hair was rolled into tight curls held in place with hair pins which slipped out as she moved so that her hands constantly flew up to push them back. Sam was reminded of her own gran, who had shared exactly the same habit.

'Good morning,' she said politely. 'Mrs Roberts? My name is Sam Rayner. I'm a friend of Will Heston. He suggested you might be able to help me.'

'Don't know what I can do. Mr Clark is away at present.'

'It's really you I want to talk to.'

'What do you want?' the woman asked defensively. 'I have work to do, you know. Can't stand here gossiping all day.'

'It's about the garden. You see, my grandfather was a nurseryman, specialising in exotic shrubs and trees, and when I walked up through the valley I couldn't help noticing that there are very many varieties of trees growing there. I thought they must have been planted for some reason and I wondered if there are any old documents? I'd be most interested to learn something of the history of this place.'

'I couldn't let anything go out of the house. Not without Mr Clark's permission,' Mrs Roberts said uncertainly.

'Of course not,' Sam agreed.

'You're not from round here, are you?' Mrs Roberts accused her.

Sam explained a little more about herself.

'Oh, so you work for Lucinda Johns, do you? You'd best come in then.' It seemed that she had provided sufficient information for acceptance.

She walked into what had once been a magnificent entrance hall, now spoiled by a huge expanse of plastic sheeting fastened along the entire length of one side. She could see builders' debris on the other side and could hear the cheery whistling of the workers accompanying loud radio music.

'I don't know what things are coming to. All this noise and upset,' Mrs Roberts grumbled as she shuffled along the hall. She opened a baize-covered door, a touch of elegance quite out of place with the present surroundings. 'I was about to have some coffee. I'll make you a cup as well.' It was a statement rather than an offer.

Sam smiled. 'Thank you. That's most kind of you.'

'Doesn't mean I can let you have anything to take away,' the woman added sharply. 'Mr Clark would be most upset if I allowed a stranger into the place.'

'Perhaps I could speak to him myself,' Sam suggested.

'Don't know when he'll be back. I'll get the coffee. You'd best sit down.'

The kitchen was huge. The long pine table was well-used and Sam could imagine kitchen-maids cursing the vast area that needed daily scrubbing. There was a solid fuel cooker in an alcove to one side and rather old-fashioned cupboards covered the walls. The largest freezer she had ever seen stood on the opposite side of the room and a huge fridge near to it.

Despite the first impression of an old, traditional kitchen, there were labour-saving appliances, including a microwave and a large electric mixer. Freezers and convenience foods must have replaced the whole team of servants once needed.

The housekeeper banged a heavy kettle on to one of the hotplates and picked up a tray which she covered with an immaculate embroidered traycloth. On it she set out china cups and saucers and plates. Delicious home-baked shortbread was brought out of a tin and three triangles were carefully placed on a doyley-covered plate. Sam was reminded of the afternoon teas of childhood, whenever she and her brother had visited their gran.

'This is really very kind of you,' she said politely.

'Now then, you'd better tell me again exactly what it is you want.'

Sam did her best to explain what was little more than some fantasy she had been developing in her mind. Spoken aloud, her ideas of discovering and restoring the garden wilderness sounded quite ridiculous.

Mrs Roberts pursed her lips and reached a decision. 'I think there may be some old books in one of the store-rooms. I don't suppose there's any harm in you looking. Come on — I'll take you through.'

'It's very good of you. I do appreciate

it.' Sam followed the woman back through the heavy baize door. 'How long have you worked here?'

'Most of my life. My parents worked here. My mother was a parlour-maid and Dad worked in the gardens before the war. The Great War I mean. He came back wounded and they moved down to Pengelly village. I was born in the twenties. When they died, I came here to be a sort of caretaker. Mr Roberts was a general handyman. But he passed on ten years back. I didn't have anywhere else to go and stayed on here. It's all change these days, though. Nothing seems to stay the same.'

The woman led her up some stairs at the back of the kitchen. She pulled a bunch of keys from her pocket and fumbled with the lock of a small room.

'Nobody's been in here in months. I don't know what you're looking for, but you can have a rummage round. I'll be in the kitchen if you want me.'

'Thanks very much,' Sam said absently, already focussing on the heaps of boxes piled on the floor among old furniture, lampshades and other oddments.

It was dusty and the dim light made it difficult to see much, but as her eyes grew accustomed to the gloom, she pulled out the first of the boxes. There were a few old books but nothing to do with the house or garden.

Several boxes later, she came across some old household accounts. It was fascinating stuff, with bills for all manner of things. It must have been a grand house, years ago, with many servants. Everything was recorded in careful handwriting, some of it beautifully formed, providing evidence of a time when the pace of life had been slower. Interesting though it was, however, it still wasn't quite what she was hoping for. She burrowed further into the boxes.

Mrs Roberts came to the door of the room.

'Any luck?' she asked. 'My goodness, what a mess it all is. I should have turned out all this rubbish years ago. Never seemed to have time though.'

'Thanks very much for letting me look,' Sam said. 'I wonder — do you think I could come again? I have to get back now but I just know there must be something in here. I feel it in my bones.'

'I expect so,' Mrs Roberts replied. 'Though I'll have to ask Mr Clark, if he happens to be in touch. Now, you just make sure and give my regards to Lucinda Johns.'

Sam walked back through the wood, looking hard at the trees and shrubs. Above the tangle of undergrowth, palm trees stretched upwards, straining to reach the sunlight. Ferns were growing, some of them so high that they looked like trees themselves. Of course, she murmured, they *were* trees. Tree ferns from New Zealand. Pungas. She'd seen pictures of them.

'I must be able to do something,' she whispered to the sleeping forest.

★   ★   ★

She was unpacking a delivery in the stock-room when she heard someone come into the shop the next day.

'Is Samantha working today?' she overheard.

'Certainly is, my 'an'some. She's just checking some stock in. I'll give her a call. Sam, there's someone to see you! It's Will Heston — you know, the young gardener fellow from the Hall.'

'Oh, right. Er, thanks,' she stammered, feeling very embarrassed. She pushed a few stray fronds of hair away from her face and went out to speak to him.

'Hello, Sam,' he said. 'Sorry to interrupt but I was passing and wondered if you'd thought any more about coming for that drink?'

'Not really. Like I said, I can't leave Allie and I don't know anyone I could ask to mind her.'

'There's always me,' Lucinda chipped in. 'I'd be happy to stay with her. You go out and enjoy yourself. Do you good to get a bit of a change.'

Sam looked doubtful. She wasn't entirely sure she wanted to go out with Will, but short of being obviously rude, she could hardly refuse.

'If you're sure,' she said to Mrs Johns. 'Thanks, Will. It would be nice.'

'We could have a bite to eat as well, if you like. Save me cooking one of my instant gourmet dinners,' Will said. 'Thursday all right for you?' Lucinda nodded and Sam agreed. They arranged that he would pick up Lucinda on his way, to save her the walk up the steep cliff.

When he had gone, however, Sam immediately regretted her impulse.

'Oh dear,' she muttered, 'I hope I'm doing the right thing.'

'He's a good man, you know. You could do a lot worse,' Lucinda said with the gleam of a born matchmaker in her eye.

'He seems nice enough. He gave Allie and me a lovely day out at Flambards. Allie thinks the sun shines out of him . . . or more accurately, out of Jenny. I just don't want him to get the wrong idea about me.'

'I think he asked you out for a drink, not to marry him,' Lucinda said a trifle sharply.

'You're quite right, of course. I'm being silly. It's just that — well, he's really nice and everything, but he isn't exactly my type.'

'And what exactly is your type? Someone like that husband of yours, I expect,' Lucinda said shrewdly. Sam had told her the whole story when they had first arrived.

Sam smiled. 'I guess I'm a bit nervous at the thought of anything so close to a real date. I've completely forgotten what it's like to go out with any man, apart from my brother!'

'He's a nice chap, Will Heston. You'd go a long way to find a kinder soul.'

'You're right,' Sam agreed. 'Now, if I don't get back to checking off this order, I'll be getting the sack. My boss is very strict.'

Lucinda giggled and watched her go

through to the stock-room. She had become very fond of her new employee in so short a time. Perhaps she rekindled happy memories of days gone by.

'Come on now, Lucinda,' she muttered softly to herself. 'There's a lot more to life than hankering after the old days.'

★   ★   ★

By the time Thursday evening arrived, Sam was a bag of nerves, quite unlike anything Allie had ever seen.

'Will he kiss you, do you think?' the little girl asked innocently. 'You know, the sort of thing where they don't make any proper kissing sounds?'

'Really, Allie. Where do you get such funny ideas?'

'It was in a film. This man and lady stood by the sea one day and were being all soppy, kissing and everything.'

Sam hid a smile. Kiss Will? She hadn't given such a thing a thought.

She considered it. It might be nice, but then, wasn't that the start of 'getting involved'? That was most certainly not what she wanted.

'I shouldn't think so for a moment,' she said firmly. 'Now, do you want beans or fish fingers?'

'What do you want?' Allie asked. 'Oh no, you're going out for dinner, aren't you?'

'You can have fish,' Sam decided. She didn't want to continue this conversation any further and banged about with the grill pan. Kiss Will indeed. What an idea!

She changed into a clean pair of cream linen trousers that didn't seem to be showing their age quite as badly as she had feared. She hoped the little knitted top she chose would be warm enough and suitable for the occasion. Too bad if it wasn't. It was only a bar supper, for heaven's sake!

Will and Lucinda arrived punctually at seven-thirty. Allie was bouncing up and down with excitement. She was secretly planning to ask Will if he would let Jenny stay with her for the evening. She saw the Land-Rover stop outside and rushed to the door, but her face fell as she realised that the little dog wasn't with them.

'Where's Jenny?' she burst out, almost before the door was open.

'Allie, don't be rude,' Sam said. 'At least let them get inside first.'

'She's at home, snoozing happily in her bed. Hi. How are you?'

'We're all right. I think Mum's a bit nervous though,' she said in a loud whisper and Sam wished the floor could swallow her up.

'I shall have to look after her then, won't I?' Will said with a laugh.

'Now, bed at half-past eight,' Sam put in. 'No later. You know the rules when you have school next day.'

They finally left and, feeling very shy and rather awkward, Sam climbed into his Land-Rover.

'Sorry. I don't suppose this is the sort of transport you're used to,' Will said.

'It's fine. It gets you there. Remember, I don't have a car of any kind.'

'I'd heard you came to the Hall to look through some old junk. Mrs R was full of it. What's your interest? I must say, you're becoming almost obsessed by the old place.'

'I'm not sure. I just feel compelled, in some strange way. It seems sad to me that it fell into such decay.'

'There's only a limited amount that one man can do,' Will said defensively.

'I didn't mean to criticise you. I sense it was once a very special place and I'd love to find something of that other world. It's as if there's a story lying hidden away, waiting to be uncovered.'

'And you're the person to uncover it?' Will remarked, his eyes crinkling as he smiled. 'Well, I don't think our Mr Clark will be remotely interested. If it doesn't make stacks of money, forget it.'

They spent a pleasant, companionable evening in the delightful little pub. It was used mostly by the locals and slightly too far from a major car park to tempt the visitors to walk there. Local fish was the speciality and Sam found herself enjoying the evening far more than she had been expecting. Before either of them realised, it was ten-thirty.

'I should be getting back,' she sighed. 'I don't like to keep Lucinda up too late. It's been a lovely evening though. Thank you.'

'My pleasure. I've enjoyed it too. We should do it again.' He smiled and stood up. 'I'll settle the bill and we can get back to rescue Lucinda from the clutches of your daughter.'

She watched him as he strode across the little room. He moved with the natural grace of someone used to hard, physical work. He was a reserved man who conveyed little of his thoughts. They had chatted easily throughout the evening, but she still knew nothing about what made him tick.

Back at the cottage, Lucinda was dozing in front of the TV news. She woke with a start and sat up.

'I must have nodded off,' she

apologised. 'I'm so sorry.'

'Don't worry about it. Allie's quite capable of coming to find anything she wants. It was just a case of being sure she wasn't left alone. Thank you so much for staying with her.'

'Any time. I mean it, Sam. I've enjoyed being with her. She's a delightful child. I hope it's done you good to get out for a bit of a change.' As she picked up her bag and went to the door, Will turned to smile at Sam.

'Thanks for coming,' he said, reaching out a hand to touch her arm. He gave it a slight squeeze and turned to follow Lucinda.

Sam waved as she went back inside. Since her daughter's comment about kissing Will, she had subconsciously been wondering all evening what on earth she would do if he did attempt to kiss her. Now that he hadn't, it was a feeling of relief rather than disappointment. Nice though he was, Will Heston was unlikely to turn into any sort of romantic entanglement for her.

Buried Treasure

'What did you have for dinner, Mum?' asked Allie the next morning.

'Was it nice? Are you going out with Will again?'

'Now which question shall I answer first?' laughed Sam. 'Hurry up and finish your toast.'

'Did you have a nice time?' repeated Allie.

'Very nice, thank you. Now, school.'

'Do you think you'll get married and live happily ever after?'

'Things don't happen like that. Will's very nice but we're only friends.'

A slow smile crossed Allie's face. 'We'll see. Bye, Mum.' She waved, the cheeky grin still on her face.

We'll see indeed, thought Sam. She had never realised that her daughter harboured such thoughts.

She had a couple of hours off and

planned to go back to Pengelly Hall.

'Oh, it's you again,' Mrs Roberts greeted her gruffly, her face unsmiling. 'I expect you'll be wanting to ferret around that old junk?'

'If possible,' Sam said politely.

'You'd best come in then. I haven't got time to spend talking today. I've had notice that Mr Clark's returning. Some secretary woman wrote me a letter. Said he'd be back at the end of the month but past experience tells me it could be any time.'

'Thanks. I hope you won't be in any trouble for this.'

Upstairs, she pushed open the door of the store-room and the musty smell of the room filled her nostrils. She delved down to find an old suitcase that had caught her eye last time. The catch gave way easily. Old, yellowing papers tied in bundles filled the case. Some were battered and torn and looked as if clumsy handling would cause them to crumble to nothing.

Very carefully she untied the ribbons.

There were several bills for dresses and fabrics in the first bundle. Some of the ladies had had very expensive ways and spent as much as two or three pounds on evening dresses! What a different world. The next bundle held stock lists from the kitchen. The number of home-made preserves was quite staggering.

Sam's next discovery set her heart pounding. Photographs. Sepia prints and faded pictures of gardens, flower-beds and several buildings. Carefully posed rows of people in turn-of-the-century dress stood in front of the various features. Had they all been taken in this garden?

She continued her search. What treasures! She came across the account book kept by the head gardener and grinned excitedly. This could give her many of the answers she was seeking. There were lists of plants, seeds and even the men's wages. This was better than she had dreamed possible.

A red leather-bound book lay at the

bottom of the suitcase. It was tied with a satin ribbon. She fingered it and held it to her face for a second. The scent of the leather filled her senses and she closed her eyes . . .

A new perfume surrounded her. She could smell the flowery fragrance of lavender and clean laundry. She opened her eyes and stared at the book. A sense of expectation ran through her as she removed the ribbon and gently opened the pages. Careful handwritten text lay before her. The first page bore the inscription: *'This is the most private diary of Marguerite Westcott'*.

Sam felt compelled to read it. It was as if the book had been left for her to find.

She turned the pages and discovered that Marguerite Westcott had been one of the daughters of the family. From this young girl's diary, she would get a clearer picture of her daily life and valuable information about the sleeping garden. She closed the book, wondering how she might persuade the current owner of the Hall to let her borrow it.

She bundled the papers back together leaving out the gardener's account book, the photographs and the diary. How sad that there was no-one left to care about them.

She went back to the kitchen and knocked soundlessly on the baize door.

'Mrs Roberts?' she called, pushing it open.

'Hello, my dear,' the woman replied. 'Any luck?'

'I think so. I've found several interesting things but I have to get back to work now. Do you think I could possibly take them away with me? I promise I'll take great care of them and return them as soon as I can.'

Mrs Roberts looked doubtful and Sam felt guilty.

'I'm sorry. I shouldn't have asked. Of course you can't give me permission.'

'What exactly have you found?' the woman asked and Sam showed her the bundle.

Mrs Roberts considered.

'There's no-one wants any of that old

stuff, I don't suppose. I doubt if anyone even knows it exists. You take it, dear. I'll mention it to his lordship when he comes back. As long as I know where it is, I don't see there's a problem.'

Sam smiled gratefully. She could hardly wait until she finished work.

'Sorry I'm late, Lucinda,' she apologised when she got back to the shop. 'I lost track of the time.'

'No problem, my love,' Lucinda said in her warm Cornish accent. 'I've plenty of time to catch the bus. You 'ad lunch yourself?'

Lucinda insisted on giving her a pack of fresh sandwiches as Sam was to stay until closing time.

All afternoon, Sam kept thinking of the treasures waiting at home. It felt rather like getting a new book by a favourite author.

* * *

After supper, mother and daughter sat on the floor and stared at the faded photographs. A group of ladies were pictured, standing in front of a summer-house. An ornamental pond was in front of them and a profusion of plants surrounded them.

'Wow! Fancy having to wear all those clothes in summer,' Allie said, staring at the long skirts and large hats worn by the group. 'And they're carrying umbrellas.'

'Parasols,' Sam replied. 'Ladies liked to shade themselves from the sun in those days.'

'How on earth did they manage to swim then?' Allie demanded.

The next half-hour was spent in a practical history lesson, with both of them deciding they were glad they lived today rather than then.

'Time for bed now,' Sam told her daughter, scooting her up the narrow staircase. She was longing to read the old diary of Marguerite Westcott, impossible while Allie was still around asking endless questions.

She sat curled up on the floor and

was instantly transported back in time. The author of the diary was a young girl in her teens. *'I was almost discovered today. Mrs Palmer was due to fit my dress for the summer ball. I had been sitting in the Italian garden, waiting for Henry. He was working on the opposite side of the pond. He really is very brown. I am certain everyone must hear my heart beating. Then, Rosalie spoilt everything when she came to find me. Henry looked up and touched his cap. He told her he hadn't seen me and she went away. I crept out and Henry went rather red. He didn't know I had been watching him. I had to leave in case Rosalie came back. I shall wait for him later, near the crystal cave. If only Mama and Papa could see what a wonderful man he is. They expect me to be interested in the awful young men coming down for the ball. Boring, boring.'*

Sam smiled. She could identify with the young girl's feelings. She had once thought that clothes and parties were the most exciting things, but after Martin's departure her life had changed dramatically. There were fewer invitations. She had been invited to occasional parties but she had hated being odd one out and it hadn't taken her long to learn to avoid social occasions.

She went back to the diary.

'*Mama informed us that Rosalie is to be married. She's become engaged to a captain in the army. I suppose it means we shall be spending the rest of this month in endless talk about the wedding and what everyone will wear. I and five of our cousins are to be bridesmaids.*

'*The wedding is still seven weeks away. I am not certain that I shall survive seven weeks of this wretched planning. I escape as often as I can, down into Papa's beloved jungle garden.*'

Sam was fascinated. Jungle garden, crystal cave . . . what and where were they? Tomorrow she would re-visit Pengelly Hall and maybe she and Will might look for some of the places. There must still be signs of the pond, the summer-house and the Italian garden. And the jungle garden.

★ ★ ★

'What are we doing today?' Allie asked next morning and Sam considered.

'Work this morning and I thought we might go to Pengelly after that and see if we can find any of the places in the old photos.'

'If Will and Jenny are there, that's cool. Let's take a picnic, shall we?'

'All right. Let's see what we can find for it.'

When the chores were done, they set off and soon reached the grassy meadow at the end of the wood. The old house looked empty and abandoned without the builders.

'I want to look over there,' Sam suggested. 'I think that's where the old summer-house may be. Come on.'

They pushed their way through the

bushes but huge rotten tree trunks, presumably fallen in long-forgotten storms, barred their way. After a great deal of clambering, they came to a crumbling wall. Massive growths of ivy and brambles stopped them from looking further.

'We'll never get through this lot,' Allie grumbled. 'My jeans have got ripped and I'm bleeding everywhere.' Her voice turned into a wail as she saw the long scratches on her bare arms.

'I suppose we'd better go back,' Sam conceded. 'You're right. We need something to chop our way through this lot. But I'm sure this is the right place. I think we might find the remains of an ornamental pond and maybe a summer-house beyond that wall.'

Reluctantly she turned away as Allie dashed off, her wounds forgotten. She had spotted a small white dog, burrowing through the tangle of bushes. Jenny had magic enough to cure all ills!

Crashes and the snapping of twigs indicated Allie's progress and soon Sam could hear voices. By the time she arrived, Allie had invited Will to join them for the picnic and was organising where everyone should sit.

'I hope this is OK with you?' Will asked as Sam joined them.

'And there're crisps and chocolate for afters,' Allie prattled. 'Mrs Johns gave them to me. Can I give Jenny some crisps?'

'Just one or two,' Will agreed. 'I don't want her getting any fatter or she'll get stuck down every rabbit hole.'

Sam told Will about her discoveries, especially the photographs. He offered to go with her and help with cutting back the decades' growth of weeds.

'I'll feel better if you're there,' Sam confided. 'I don't want to be accused of trespass by the elusive Mr Jackson Clark. Mrs R. said he's due back any time. Everyone had enough?' she asked, stuffing the rubbish into her rucksack. She was eager to get on with her search.

Allie, in her seventh heaven, disappeared to play with Jenny while the adults fought their way through the jungle of bushes and fallen trees, Will holding back massive trails of brambles to help Sam through.

They finally reached the wall and pushed their way along it until there was a reasonable gap. Will pulled a folding pruning knife from his pocket and began to hack away and finally, with much squeezing and pushing, they managed to get into what Sam believed was the Italian garden. Under tangled growth, she could see stone slabs. She bent down and felt the edge of what might be the ornamental pond. At one end was evidence of brickwork and even a crumbling building. This had to be the right place. She closed her eyes and remembered the old photograph.

'Well?' Will asked. 'Found what you were looking for?'

'I think so. I really think so!' Sam was imagining clear water, alive with gold-fish and water lilies. Surrounding it would be exotic herbaceous borders. The summer-house dominated the little formal garden. She could even imagine the young Marguerite hiding behind one of the walls as she watched her gardener working. 'I'm certain this is the site in the old photograph. Isn't it exciting?' she said.

He smiled at her obvious enthusiasm and reached for a hand but she turned away.

'It's all right, Sam, I don't bite,' he told her with a wry look.

She stared at him, lost for words. No man had looked at her in that way for years. She didn't want to be involved, yet she could feel herself being drawn inexorably towards him.

'I should go and find Allie,' she said feebly. 'I don't want her to get lost.'

She felt Will's eyes burning into the back of her as she turned away. She didn't need complications at this time. Will would have to be involved if there was any way she could achieve her fantasy of restoring this garden, and a personal relationship might get in the way.

'Allie,' she called and Jenny came dashing out, wagging her tail, followed by Allie.

'Hi, Mum. I'm having the best fun! Jenny's such a good little dog. Did you know she can sit up and beg? She's very clever. She knows exactly what I say. Oh, did you find the garden thingy?'

'Yes, I think it's safe to say we found the garden *thingy*, don't you?' she asked with an amused glance at Will.

'I'm sure we did. Now, where to next?'

'Shall we just wander and see what else we can find?' she suggested.

'There are old paths everywhere but they're totally overgrown,' he warned.

'Where was the jungle garden?' she asked, suddenly remembering the diary.

'I think that must have been in the valley. Some of the old locals in the pub mentioned Westcott's jungle. Well-known for the variety of exotic trees from all over the world, they say.'

'So that's what my forest is. Why didn't you mention it earlier?'

'I'd forgotten the old name until you asked. There were lakes and waterfalls, I believe. They're mostly dried up now, apart from a few muddy patches.'

Sam gave a shiver of excitement. She remembered slipping down a muddy track. Water must still find some way to flow through the valley.

'Now,' Will said, 'can Jenny and I tempt you to come home with me for some tea? Believe I owe you a cup.'

'Yes, please,' Allie said before her mother could speak. Anything to spend more time with the little dog and their new friend.

'I can drive you back afterwards,' he added.

'Great,' Allie declared. 'My legs couldn't possibly manage to walk me all the way back home.'

Sam marvelled again at her child's assurance. Whatever anyone said about modern-day education, it gave children plenty of confidence.

★ ★ ★

Will's home was a small, pretty lodge, built of the same stone as the main house. The garden was a riot of colour with early roses climbing over trellis screens.

'Oh, this is lovely!' Sam said with enthusiasm. 'What a picture!'

'Thanks,' Will replied. 'I'd like to make the Hall's garden look as good but it's impossible. Come on in. I'll put the kettle on.'

Allie peered round with unashamed curiosity.

'Where does Jenny sleep?' was her first question.

Once she had familiarised herself with Jenny's entire lifestyle, she went out into the garden to play ball with the little dog.

Will smiled. 'It's easy to see why I'm so popular. It's my dog that's the winner.'

He made tea and put out a plate of cakes and shortbread. Sam thought she recognised Mrs Robert's hand in the baking. The whole place was as clean as a new pin, surprisingly neat and tidy, comfortable and homely.

'This is nice,' Sam said. 'Do you have help with the cleaning?'

'Of course not,' he replied. 'There's only me and I don't make much mess. Besides, it's had its Saturday morning blitz. Now, cake or shortbread?'

'How long have you lived here?' she asked conversationally.

'I moved back eight years ago.' His jaw tightened and he was obviously remembering something unpleasant. Sam said nothing but made a mental note to ask Lucinda what she knew. 'I'd better call Allie or she'll miss out on tea.'

He went into the garden and Sam took the chance to look around the room. There were no pictures, no photographs. It felt as if something were missing.

Will and Allie came back, the little girl holding his hand comfortably. She perched on a stool and took the plate and cake she was offered. Between bites of her cake, she prattled on about Jenny and the amazing things the dog could do, and Sam relaxed, happy to let her daughter take charge of the conversation. She glanced at Will and saw that he was staring at the child with an odd expression. He was looking at her almost as though he were wishing she was someone else.

'We ought to be getting back,' Sam said at last. 'Thanks for the tea and for helping find the Italian garden.'

'I promised to drive you,' Will reminded her. 'Do you want to come again tomorrow? See what else we can find?'

'Yes, thank you. We'd like that, wouldn't we, Mum?' Allie said quickly.

'Well, I don't want to take up too much of your time,' Sam began.

'Tell you what — why not come for lunch and then we can continue our exploration during the afternoon?' he urged.

'We couldn't impose,' Sam protested but Allie interrupted.

'We'd love to, thank you very much. Mum can never make her mind up.' She ignored the warning glance from her mother.

'Good. That's settled then. I'll pick you up at noon and save you the walk. I specialise in Sunday roasts ... an experience not to be missed.' If Will had felt rejected back in the garden, he wasn't showing it. If only they could be friends and not complicate matters with anything more, she mused.

He dropped them off at their cottage and Allie hugged Jenny, promising to see her the next day. To Sam's amazement, she also gave Will a hug and kissed him on the cheek before they waved him off.

'You do like him, don't you, Mummy?' Allie asked anxiously.

'Of course I do. But you mustn't be too pushy, darling. I know you love little Jenny but don't get carried away by your enthusiasm.'

'It's no different from your enthusiasm for the garden,' Allie pointed out with almost adult reasoning. 'I'm going up to my room for a bit.'

Funny child, Sam thought. Perhaps she, too, needed more male company.

Will was only being kind to them both, she reminded herself. Maybe it was time she tried to break out of her self-imposed loneliness now that Martin was dead. But the hurt of his leaving had made her too scared to risk any new relationship. Besides, there had always been Allie to consider. She had never dared let a third person into their lives in case it caused the little girl any more suffering.

But this was not the time for daydreaming. She had work to do and the delightful prospect of more diary to read.

'We're to have white crêpe de Chine dresses with satin sashes ... blue, I think. Everyone is so busy, they don't notice when I go out for my walks. Henry tells me he will get into trouble if I keep stopping him from working. I'm certain he likes me. I'm sure he wants to kiss me but dare not. The village girls all kiss the men and they all seem to like it. I wonder what it really feels like to be so close to someone?'

Sam smiled. How innocent it sounded. A teenager in those times would be unlike any today. She continued to read. The wedding came and went. A feast was prepared for all the workers in what she called the sundial garden. The expense of creating a garden like that would be quite prohibitive today. Her secret ambition to restore the garden would take a great deal of time, effort and a fantastic amount of money. It was all a ridiculous dream.

She put the diary to one side and took out the photographs, hoping there might be one of Rosalie's wedding. But there were none. There was a picture of a man in a bowler hat, standing formally among some bushes. Could he be the young gardener Henry, mentioned by the adoring Marguerite? She shut her eyes, imagining the world where rank within the servant hierarchy made so much difference to the way of life.

Equality was something she herself felt strongly about, and from Marguerite's words, she had probably felt very much the same, which would not have sat easily with her parents who were obviously very conscious of rank and status.

She noticed a picture of a young woman standing in front of a sundial, surrounded by immaculate green lawns and flower beds. The sundial. Perhaps it still existed somewhere under all the rubbish. Sam looked again. This woman was wearing more modern clothing. It must have been taken at a much later date than the others. Odd. How had it found its way amongst the rest of the pictures?

If she could only find an old plan of the garden, she would have a better idea of where to start looking. Maybe there was someone still living locally who could help her to find out more information? Lucinda Johns had lived in the area all her life. Perhaps she would know of someone.

Lunch the next day was a great success. Will hadn't been exaggerating when he'd claimed to specialise in roast dinners. He had cooked lamb with fresh potatoes and beans from his garden. Perfect mint sauce and gravy accompanied the meal.

'Why don't you cook Sunday lunches like this, Mum?' Allie asked.

'Wouldn't be such a treat if we had it every week.' Sam bit her lip. Her cooking wasn't nearly up to this standard. She would be hard pressed to produce such a meal when and if she invited Will back.

There was apple pie for pudding, served with Cornish clotted cream.

'Wow, that's me finished for days,' she announced, finally putting her spoon down. 'Wonderful meal, Will. Thank you so much. Now, Allie and I will do the washing up.'

'Nonsense. You'll sit down while I make coffee. I have a dishwasher in any case.'

'Fancy having a dishwasher just for one person,' Allie said, her eyes wide.

They relaxed, chatting comfortably with each other. Allie and Jenny went to play ball outside and excited barks and the girl's voice could be heard.

'Is there anything particular we're looking for this afternoon?' Will asked.

Sam took the sundial photograph out of her bag to show him, and he came to sit on the arm of her chair and peered over her shoulder. She could feel his warm breath on the side of her neck. He leaned over to point at something, and their heads were very close. He looked at her, then gently put a finger under her chin and brushed her lips with his . . .

Before she could make any movement, he rose again, cutting short the brief moment. Sam didn't know whether she felt glad or sorry.

'So, do you think you know where the sundial is?' she asked.

'Haven't a clue,' Will replied. 'I have enough to do in the garden near the house. Everywhere else is running riot. Shall we see what we can find though?'

It was a weary, rather dirty trio that finally drove back to Sam's cottage.

'Thanks again, Will,' she said as they stopped outside. 'We've had a lovely day.'

He leaned over and gave her a peck on the cheek, then did the same to Allie as she got out of the back of the Land-Rover. She put her arms round his neck and whispered to him.

'You're really nice, Will, and I think Jenny is the best dog in the whole world.'

Will's expression flickered with sadness but he forced a smile.

'Thank you, Allie. You're pretty special too. See you soon.'

He drove away with a wave of his hand.

Big Plans

It was a couple of days before Sam had time to re-visit her obsession, as she had begun to call it. She walked up through the valley and struck off to the left a little way before reaching the open lawn near the house. Soon, she reached another old wall.

'Who's there?' shouted an unfamiliar voice. Through the vegetation, she could make out a shape and a flash of blue denim.

'It's me, Sam — Samantha Rayner,' she called back, thinking it must be one of the workmen. She put out her hand as the stranger drew closer and he reciprocated and smiled.

'Well, Samantha Rayner, tell me what you're doing here.' His voice was quiet and well modulated. Nor did he have any trace of the local accent common to most of the builders. He was taller than her, with dark hair, greying very slightly at the temples. Intelligent grey-blue eyes stared at her.

'I found some old photographs of the garden,' she explained. 'I'm trying to find some of the places in the pictures. It must have been an amazing place at one time.'

'Show me what you've found,' he asked.

Sam gave a shrug and turned towards the entrance of what she now thought of as the Italian garden.

'There — I think that's an old ornamental pond and there's the summer-house.'

'Good heavens,' said the stranger. 'You could be right. What other treasures do you think are waiting?'

'I think there was a flower garden, with a sundial in the middle. That's what I'm looking for this afternoon.'

'Let's see if we can find it then, shall we?'

Sam was delighted to find someone else showing an interest. They pushed their way towards the old mellow brick wall, rather painfully at times. Struggling along it, at last they came to a battered old gate, a doorway set into an arch in the wall. Sam's chest constricted in excitement. What lay beyond this gate? Could it be the sundial garden?

Together they heaved to push it open, but something was blocking it from the other side and however hard they pushed, it wouldn't budge. Disappointment swept through her. So near and yet so far.

'We might have to get a ladder and go over the top, but let's give it one more try,' the man said.

Together they leaned against the door once more, bracing their legs against the ground to increase the pressure.

'I think it may be moving,' he said breathlessly.

An inch, another, and it gave way. They pushed enough of a gap to peer through.

Everything was buried under weeds

and the rotting timbers of what may have been a greenhouse rested against the wall.

'I don't think this is your flower garden,' the man said. 'Fruit or greenhouse crops, I'd say.'

'This whole place is quite amazing,' breathed Sam.

'So, Samantha Rayner, is this what you were hoping to discover. If so, why?'

'You'll think I'm potty,' she said defensively, knowing that this would be the first time she was actually going to voice her dreams for this place.

'Try me.'

'Well, I dream of seeing all this restored to its former glory. Can't you imagine the gardens as a working historical site from Victorian days? Any history of the place seems very sketchy. Not even the locals remember much. Mrs Roberts, the housekeeper, let me look through some old boxes. There were a few photos and some accounts. I've been to the local library, but they have nothing. All we know is that everything went to sleep after the First World War. The team of gardeners were lost and the garden with them.' Her voice tailed away.

'It's an interesting idea, but how on earth could you tackle a project this size? It would be an enormous task. Do you know anything about gardens?'

She filled him in on her background, and found herself telling him her reasons for moving to Cornwall, her meetings with Will Heston and even about her childhood memories of the area.

'And do you also believe in fate?' he asked, a flicker of a grin playing at the corner of his mouth. He was teasing her and she didn't like it.

'You asked me and I told you,' she said coldly. 'I know it sounds crazy but just imagine all this, restored and working again. People would come for miles to see it. But I'm dreaming, I know. Who are you, anyway?'

'Clark,' he said. 'I'm Jackson Clark. I

happen to own all this.'

Sam blushed with embarrassment. 'I'm sorry . . . I didn't realise . . . I thought you were one of the workmen, an architect or someone. I'll bring back the papers and things I borrowed just as soon as I can.'

'How very fairytale — mistaking the rich and handsome prince for one of the workmen.' He grinned, amused. 'But there's no hurry to return anything. I'd like to think about what you've said. Why not come over for dinner this evening? We can talk it through. Around seven, if you're free. And bring those photographs. I'd like to see them.'

'I have a young daughter. I don't have anyone who could sit with her at such short notice.' She sounded regretful. This was possibly her one golden chance and she was having to turn it down.

'Are you sure there isn't anyone who could babysit?'

'She's nine — hardly a baby. Maybe I

could ask Lucinda Johns. But I don't like to take advantage.'

'See what you can do. I'll give you my mobile number. I don't know where I'll be for the rest of the afternoon.' He scribbled the number on a scrap of paper and she tucked it in her pocket, then glanced at her watch. 'Heavens, I'll have to hurry. My daughter's due home from school any minute.'

'I'd better drive you then. My car's round the front. Then I can wait while you ask Mrs whatever if she'll sit for you.'

Sam had no choice and accepted the lift gratefully. Allie would already be at home.

As they drove into the village, she saw Allie, walking back down the hill towards the shop. The expression on her face changed from one of slight irritation to sheer amazement when the sleek red car pulled up beside her and her mother got out.

'So who's your *friend* today?' she asked with mock severity.

'Allie, this is Mr Clark. He owns Pengelly Hall.'

He reached his hand out towards her and shook hers formally.

'I came across your mother trespassing and had to chase her off my land.'

'I'm sorry, Mr Clark. She's awful. She's always doing it. Mr Heston's already told her off.' Allie's expression was equally humourless and Sam found herself suddenly laughing.

Jackson Clark grinned. 'I see. I'm glad you warned me. Well, once you've arranged your young lady-sitter, I'll get back and organise Mrs Roberts.'

Sam turned and went into the shop, where she found Lucinda waiting inside the door, bursting with curiosity about the flashy car and its occupant.

'You're certainly going up in the world.' She laughed. 'Who is it this time?'

'Lucinda, I wouldn't dream of asking you if it wasn't so important, but do you think you could possibly sit for us this evening? That's Mr Clark who owns the Hall and he's invited me to dinner.'

'Oh, has he now?' she said, disapproval gushing out of every pore.

'I told him about my discoveries and he's interested. Just imagine, Lucinda — what if that wonderful garden could be restored? There would be work for dozens of villagers again.'

'I don't want you two-timing Will Heston,' she snapped.

'Two-timing . . . ?' Sam gasped. 'I'm not. I mean, Will and I are just friends. Anyhow, Mr Clark is . . . well, it's a business meeting. Oh, never mind — I'll tell him I can't manage dinner.'

'Wait on. All right — if it's so important to you, I'll come and sit with Allie.'

'Thank you, Lucinda. Thank you so much. I'll see you later . . . as early as you can manage. I'll make something for your supper.'

She whirled and ran out of the shop, as excited as a teenager.

'It's all fixed,' she told Clark, 'though

I won't make it by seven. I don't have a car and the shop doesn't close until half-six.'

Jackson arranged to collect her, then turned the car expertly and drove away. It purred in contrast to the familiar banging and rattling of Will's Land-Rover.

'Neat car,' Allie remarked. 'I could get used to something like that.'

Sam laughed, then groaned. 'I have to find something half decent to wear if I'm dining at the Hall.'

'And I thought we were moving here for a quiet life. Two men in less than a week. I shall become a disturbed child if you're not careful!' her daughter remarked.

Life was certainly changing, Sam thought happily.

She put some chicken pieces into a casserole and added vegetables, and put it in the oven. Right now she had a much greater crisis to sort out. What was the right thing to wear for dinner at Pengelly Hall? Admittedly the place was only a shadow of its former glory, but she didn't imagine it would be a casual meal and she wanted to impress. This was the chance of a lifetime. If she could sell her idea to this man, who could tell where it might lead?

Somewhere, she knew, she had a long skirt. It was ancient but with an iron and the right top, it would just about do.

Allie watched critically as she dressed. 'If you're starting a social life, you'd better do something about your wardrobe. It's a disaster. That skirt's past it.'

'It's pretty awful, isn't it? I'm just not used to going out.'

'You didn't have this problem with Will. You were ready in five minutes flat.'

'This is different. It's business.'

Allie shrugged. Someone with a cool car like Mr Clark may well be worth a second look, though if her mother ever suspected her secret plans, she would be furious. Allie had reached a decision. It was high time she had a new father.

It was up to her to make sure her mother found her a new dad.

Mr Clark had a nice car and Pengelly Hall was a wicked place, though Jenny put Will streets ahead. Still, if they lived at the Hall, she'd be able to see Jenny every day. Yes, maybe she needed to give her vote to Jackson Clark, even if she couldn't imagine him going on the rides at Flambards.

'Wear that blouse thing with the skirt. It makes your eyes look dead blue and it'll go quite well.'

Sam looked worried. 'Are you sure?'

Allie nodded. She had enough understanding, even at nine, to realise that her mother needed reassurance.

'You'll look fine. Why don't you put your hair up as well? Save you having to wash it again. Besides, there'll probably be candles. Really rich people often try to save electricity so they can stay rich. You'll probably look all right by candlelight.'

Sam smiled and glanced at her watch. Lucinda would be here at any moment and she still had to lay the table.

'It's OK — I'll lay the table,' Allie offered, reading her mind.

★   ★   ★

It was the first time Sam had been anywhere in the Hall, except for the kitchen and store-room. Jackson's apartment was on the second floor, the numerous windows allowing views over the garden towards the distant sea.

The main room, once the library, was long with oak panelling and a polished wooden floor. Bright rugs were scattered near to the large armchairs and sofas. The light cream coverings contrasted with the darker walls, giving a feeling of comfort, even cosiness, to the lovely room. Several vases of flowers stood on pedestals, adding colour and fragrance. Not exactly the sort of surroundings one expected for a man living on his own. Presumably it was due to Mrs Roberts. She knew exactly how things should be done in the big house.

The oak dining-table was set with polished silver and cut-crystal wine glasses. There were several candles, in rather ostentatious candelabra. It all looked most imposing. Sam smoothed her rather elderly skirt, hoping she didn't look too out of place. Jackson had changed from his denims into an open-necked, soft cream shirt and grey trousers. Casually dressed, he still made an imposing figure.

'What will you have to drink?' he asked.

'Something soft, please. Orange juice or mineral water?' She needed to keep a clear head.

'So, tell me about your thoughts on my garden. Or should I call it jungle?'

Sam produced the photographs and he sat next to her on one of the large sofas. She had assumed he was much older than her but she realised it was because of the grey hair at his temples. The keen grey-blue eyes were studying the pictures.

'Interesting,' he said at last. 'Do you seriously think it's possible? I didn't realise most of it existed.'

'From what I gather, you haven't been here much,' she commented.

'My interests are elsewhere, though I'm considering living here full-time. I'll keep my flat in London, of course, but things are pretty well-organised there. I can run the business from here if necessary. Technology is a wonderful thing. And this might give me a new interest. I'll have a lot to learn. I barely know a tomato bush from a rose.'

'But would you really be interested in working on something as basic as a garden?'

'*You're* obviously interested. Go on, sell it to me.'

Sam's enthusiasm gave her confidence and she found herself confessing thoughts that had been hidden deep within her. She painted word pictures of another age, things she had learned from the diary of a young girl born over a century ago. Her passion for the project was growing by the minute. Perhaps this was why fate had driven her to Cornwall.

'Dinner's ready, sir,' Mrs Roberts announced, entering the room after knocking. For a local woman born and bred, the housekeeper would not have been out of place in any of the great houses of the past.

'Samantha,' he said politely. 'Are you ready to eat?'

'Thank you,' she replied shyly.

'I hope you don't mind my using your full name. It's not quite as masculine as the shortened version.'

'I suppose it's a relic from childhood. You're only called by your full name when your parents are cross with you.' She felt her colour rising. He had a knack of making her feel unusually feminine. She was glad she had put on a skirt instead of her standard trousers.

The meal was delicious. Simple and well-cooked, there was plenty of fresh, local produce. Once their plates were full, he urged her to talk about her plans.

'OK, I'm sold. What's the next move?' he said suddenly, as they reached the coffee stage of the meal.

'What do you mean?'

'You've sold your idea to me. We'll do it.'

She stared at him incredulously. 'You must realise it'll cost an absolute fortune! And it'll be a colossal amount of work. We'd probably have to employ great teams of people. Not to mention equipment. I'm talking big-time expenses. It's no small undertaking.'

'Are you chickening out?' he said with a serious expression.

'Of course not. But I expected you'd want to think about it for weeks. You need to get experts.'

'No, you'll organise all that. You're in charge. Will can help you. I'll provide the financial backing. Do the business plan. I'll get you a computer and we'll sort out an office for you. There's plenty of space here. I've kept most of this wing intact. Oh, and you'd better have a vehicle. It takes too long to get anywhere from here. Which would be best? Car or van? I take it you do drive?'

'Well, yes,' Sam said hesitantly. 'I can drive, but I know nothing about computers. Though I s'pose I'm not bad at typing.'

'No problem then, you'll soon pick it up, with me to help. It's essential. We can keep in touch by email when I'm away.'

She felt numb. Everything was moving too fast. Her fantasy was being taken seriously by someone who had apparently unlimited resources.

'Right. Would you prefer to organise a car or shall I do it? We'll make a start tomorrow and once you have something on paper, we can get things moving with the planning people. I have to be away for a couple of weeks but then I'll move down. We'll probably be eligible for various grants, but I'll look into that when you have definite proposals.'

'Hold on. I have a job. I can't drop

everything just like that!' she protested.

'How much notice do you have to give?'

'It isn't that simple. My cottage is part of the deal and I couldn't leave Lucinda in the lurch. She's been a good friend to me.' She felt herself being torn. He was offering the chance of a lifetime. How could she turn it down?

'Well, you need to work out your priorities. You have the enthusiasm and the idea has huge potential. It could make a lot of money and provide jobs for the area. I'm backing you all the way. Think it over seriously and I'll meet you in the walled garden, say around two tomorrow?'

'Are you always this impulsive? Don't you need to think about it?'

'If a decision's right, why waste time thinking?'

She felt as though she was being sucked into some wild, crazy dream, some impossible wish that was spiralling out of control. She had a fantastic idea of rebuilding a lost garden and now this man had arrived from nowhere, promising to make her dream come true. How on earth would she tell Lucinda about his proposition? Where would they live if she gave up her work in the shop?

'How did it go, this business meeting of yours?' Lucinda asked, a hint of ice in her voice, once Jackson had delivered Sam back to the cottage.

'I'm not sure really. He's all in favour of rebuilding the garden. Seems very enthusiastic and wants me to take charge of it. But it's all much too hurried for my liking. I don't think he even begins to understand the enormity of it all. I was planning something small-scale, a slow, gradual discovery. But he's planning to launch straight into the whole thing.'

'So I'd better start looking for a new shop assistant, had I?' the old lady suggested, her pursed lips showing her disapproval.

'Oh, Lucinda, I don't know. I thought we were so well settled here.

And he's so high-powered, I don't know if he's got the soul for such a sensitive project. Do you know anything about him? What's the gossip?

'He's not the sort of man people gossip about, though there were a few rumours flying around when he first bought Pengelly. He's supposed to have made his fortune in computers. Fought hard for a good deal on the Hall and beat down the builders' estimates to rock bottom. They say each apartment's going to cost a fortune. My guess is that he thinks the profits will be even better if he does up the grounds.

'Be careful, my lovely. Don't get in too deep. I doubt Mr Clark is much good at caring for people. My guess is that he would get rid of you just as quickly, if he changes his mind. And I couldn't keep this place vacant for you.'

'Of course not, I wouldn't expect it. I'm just not sure if I can manage everything though. I'd like to stay on at the shop for a while, and at the cottage, if I may. But I have the feeling that he'll expect at least twenty-five hours' work a day!'

'We'll talk some more tomorrow.' Lucinda hauled herself out of the chair and picked up the battered straw hat that was her summer outdoor uniform.

'Thanks again, Lucinda,' Sam said gratefully. 'Sorry I can't see you home.'

'No worries.' The woman walked off down the hill, back to her own place, her thoughts troubled. She had grown very fond of her new young friends. She would be sad to lose them, but it might throw Sam and Will together. Lucinda had high hopes of that little relationship. There may have been a few gaps in his life, times when Will had been mysteriously absent and the gossips had had a field day. No-one knew what he'd been doing, but he was a local lad and deserved only the best in Lucinda's book.

Sam lay awake for most of the night. How could she possibly fulfil her plans for Pengelly without risking the loss of what little she already had?

She felt irritable the next morning and was unnecessarily sharp with Allie.

'But I only wanted to know if you'd had a nice time,' wailed Allie. 'I s'pose it was awful and you looked all wrong in such a posh place.'

'What I looked like was nothing to do with anything,' Sam snapped. 'Anyhow, I thought you had given your royal approval to what I was wearing?'

Allie looked away. She sensed something was wrong.

'Has he got a dog?' she asked.

'Who, Jackson? No. Now hurry or you'll miss the bus. If I'm not here when you get back, wait for me at the shop.'

'He's got a very cool car and he must have pots of dosh. He could easily afford to buy a dog. Bye, Mum. See you tonight.' The girl ran out of the house. Perhaps she should concentrate on Will after all, she thought. Cool cars weren't everything.

'What Is He To You?'

When she finished her shift at one o'clock, Sam left the shop with a heavy heart. Her mind was still in turmoil but she had to keep her appointment with Jackson Clark.

She felt the peace enveloping her as she climbed through her valley. Had she ever had any real doubts in her mind?

Crowbars and shears lay on the ground near the door they had opened just a crack, and she felt a pang of disappointment. She had wanted to be there, to be a part of every discovery.

She pushed, but the door didn't budge. She picked up one of the levers and tried to prise away the piece of wooden beam that was blocking the way, but it was too heavy for her. A pair of arms came round her and strong hands grabbed the metal bar. Under the increased strength the beam shattered and the door gave way.

'Thanks,' she said, turning to look at the man behind her.

'I assumed this would be your first priority,' Jackson said with a smile. 'I got Will to bring the tools over this morning but I warned him not to try to open it. I thought you would be angry if you weren't here.'

'I would too,' Sam replied with a grin, feeling ridiculously pleased that he'd had the sensitivity to realise the importance to her of each discovery.

'Right. Let's see what there is to find.' Gently he pushed her in front of him, allowing her to be the first to step inside.

The weeds stood in land they had made their own territory. Tall foxgloves were festooned with ivy and fought for space among hundreds of other weeds. The walls enclosed a space of probably a hundred yards square. Fallen timbers lay everywhere and shards of broken glass crunched beneath their feet.

Indications of paths and stone slabs lay among the debris. An occasional dip in the ground suggested sites of greenhouses. On the opposite side was another door set into the mellow brickwork.

'I wonder where that goes?' she murmured. 'I doubt if we can get all the way across without cutting back some of this growth.'

'Maybe we should start to make some sort of map,' he suggested. 'A diagram to show how it all links up. It's so hard to know where we are without a plan.'

'Maybe we should fly over it in a balloon or something,' Sam said with a laugh.

'Good thinking. I can't do a balloon, but I do have access to a helicopter.'

'A helicopter? You're kidding me!'

'We could film the whole lot. Valley, house, walled gardens, everything. Do a proper aerial survey. It will give us something to work on. I'll get it organised.' He glanced at his watch. 'Bit late today but first thing in the morning. OK with you?'

'I'm working in the morning,' she said, biting her lip as she always did when she was troubled.

'You have to decide on your priorities,' he said again, and his voice sounded surprisingly cold. He was a man used to getting his own way. No wonder there was no sign of a wife or family around.

'I've never been in a helicopter,' she said. 'It sounds like a brilliant idea though. It would really give us a better idea of the layout.'

'Let's go back to the house. There's no point in trying to fight our way through this lot. I'll make some calls and get things rolling.'

He strode towards the house with Sam almost trotting to keep up with his pace.

'Ask Mrs R. to bring us some tea,' he commanded as he disappeared into his study.

He was sitting at a large desk, an

antique which looked at odds with the modern computer equipment sitting on it. He was speaking into the phone. 'Put the stills camera on board, and the video. I want to survey the property. Right — fine — yes, I'll see the workmen are clear of the area. Thanks. Bye.'

He turned back to Sam. 'Right, Samantha. Tomorrow you make your first helicopter trip. I trust that two o'clock leaves you time to fulfil your duties as Mrs Johns' indispensable assistant?'

'Thanks, yes.'

'We need to get things moving where we can.'

Sam felt just a stirring of anxiety within. Did he always bulldoze his way through life like this? No wonder he was so successful.

They spent the rest of the afternoon trying to sort out the immediate practicalities. She would keep her job at the shop and thus the cottage, and spend the rest of the time working here, a situation they would review at a later stage. She was delighted with the compromise and they drank a toast to the arrangements and to the future with cups of Earl Grey.

'I must get back for Allie, now,' she said. 'I don't like her to come home to an empty house.'

'She'll be finishing school for the summer soon. That'll free your time a bit. She can play here. I understand Mrs Roberts likes children.'

Surprisingly he seemed to have even these details worked out, and Sam was frankly astonished that he had taken notice of such things as school holidays.

★ ★ ★

'So, am I to be given notice?' Lucinda said, obviously still annoyed when Sam returned to the cottage.

'No. I've arranged to work afternoons at the Hall. I can swap things round if you need me to.'

'So it's still just a temporary arrangement, is it?'

'Oh, Lucinda, I'm doing my best not to let you down but it's the chance of a lifetime. I hope you understand. You could get a lot more trade yourself eventually.'

'It's the immediate future I'm bothered about. I might just sell the lot and be done with it.'

Feeling upset, Sam met Allie from the bus and they walked up the hill.

'I forgot to say, Mum — it's Sports Day tomorrow. You'll come, won't you? Everyone's mums and dads go to it. We could ask Will. Jenny would have to stay in the Land-Rover but she wouldn't mind, would she?'

Sam felt her heart sink. She couldn't let Jackson down.

'Oh, Allie, why didn't you say earlier? I've got plans for tomorrow.'

'At least *Will* cares about me. *You* don't care about me, not since you got into all this gardening stuff. I'm going to phone Will. I can pretend he's my dad. It isn't very nice for me, you know. You can't imagine what it's like. No father and a mother who's too busy doing stuff to attend my school special occasions.'

Sam gave a deep sigh. 'OK. I'll phone Mr Clark and tell him my plans have to be changed. I'll do it after tea. Which races are you in?'

'I'm giving out programmes. I haven't been there long enough to race. But Miss Dwyer said it's probably the most important job.'

'Oh, Allie, you're priceless! You want me to come to watch you sell programmes?'

After tea, she tried to explain about her plans for the next day. The child's eyes widened when the helicopter was mentioned.

'Wow! You lucky thing! Can I come? They'll never miss me at the sports.'

'I'm sure there will be other times. This 'garden thing', as you put it, is a sort of detective job. The helicopter will save us a great deal of time.'

'So it looks as if it all might happen, your gardening thing? It's all because of Grandpa, isn't it?' Sam considered.

'I suppose I share Grandpa's love of growing things. What about your sports? Do I phone Mr Clark?'

'It's OK. But can we ask Will and Jenny to tea tomorrow?'

'Make it Friday, and you've got a deal.'

* * *

Jackson was looking his usual immaculate self. Sam was hot from the climb.

'Sorry, I should have collected you,' he apologised. 'Still, that problem's sorted. I've ordered you a van. I thought it would prove more useful than a car. It's being delivered here tomorrow, so I can sign the documents before I leave. I'll pass the necessary paperwork to Mrs R. and you can collect it whenever you like. Now, if you're ready, we'll get over to the pad.'

'You have a helicopter pad here?'

'Sounds rather grand but it's just a small area of tarmac round at the side of the house. I often have to use the chopper.'

'Is it yours?' Sam gulped. How could anyone be that rich?

'It's owned by a friend who runs a subsidiary of one of my companies.'

The helicopter landed and Jackson waved at the pilot and shouted to Sam.

'There are headphones on the front seats. Only way we can hear each other. Keep to the front as you get in. Don't go behind the blades or the pilot can't see you. You go in the front seat. I'll work the cameras from the rear.'

Sam clambered in and the pilot reached over to shake her hand. He pointed to the headphones and she put them on. He showed her the microphone and how to work it. She smiled, feeling ready for anything.

They lifted off and began to circle above the house. She heard Jackson's voice telling the pilot, Justin, to fly right round behind the buildings, towards the sea. Then they would fly low over the grounds, taking film and photographs from as many angles as possible.

It was a whole different world. In seconds, they reached the sea. The forest looked impenetrable from above. The treetops hid all signs of paths with one continuous green canopy. They could see the tops of the walls but even the low altitude flight left details within the walls merging into another tangle of greenery. But they would have an overall plan of the area, the best they could hope for.

After several circuits, Jackson signalled that he had filmed enough and they landed.

'That was magic!' Sam said enthusiastically. 'Absolutely wonderful!'

'Glad you enjoyed it. We'll see what the stills look like later. We can go in and watch the video now, if you like.'

Sam glanced at her watch. It was already after three but she couldn't resist.

It was difficult to see what was

hidden within the walls of the garden. Jackson frowned. 'We're going to need some proper maps of the area. I'll order them. Come in here and use my computer while I'm away. Feel free to use it for anything you need!'

Sam blanched. 'I'm sorry, Jackson, but I don't even know how to switch one on.'

'You are joking, aren't you?' Sam shook her head miserably. 'Then I'll have to give you a crash course when I'm back. Can't get anywhere without keeping up to date with technology.'

'I think I'm more of a dirty-hands person, out there doing the digging and all that.'

Jackson gave her one of his rare grins. 'I'll bet you are. I'd hate to be a dandelion in the wrong place with you around.'

On the drive back, Sam tried hard to discover something of the man she was about to work for. He wasn't easily drawn. She tried asking blatantly if he had a wife.

'Why would you want to know that?' he asked with wry smile. 'Does it make any different to our relationship?'

'If you can call it a relationship,' Sam replied bluntly.

'I hope so, since we'll be working closely together. But I'm not the marrying kind,' he said as he opened her door. 'Always too busy. See you in a couple of weeks.'

★ ★ ★

'How was it?' Allie asked excitedly when she clambered off the school bus. 'I kept looking out to see if you would fly over Sports Day.'

'How were the programmes?' Sam asked.

'Good. When the programmes had all gone, I was in charge of the coloured bands. Everyone had to wear them for the races. It's a good job you didn't come. I wouldn't have had any time to spare for you.'

Sam stifled a grin. 'I'm glad you

didn't miss me. We made a video of the flight. You'll be able to see it soon.'

'Have you phoned Will? Is he coming for tea tomorrow?'

'We'll do it now. Oh yes — guess what we're getting tomorrow?'

'Not a dog? Oh, Mummy, is it a dog?'

'Well, no. We're getting a van. I'll be able to drive us up to Pengelly and anywhere else we want to go. Not quite as good as a dog but it'll certainly save a lot of time.'

Will wasn't in when they phoned so they left a message. They decided to make cakes ready for the next day. Even if Will didn't come, they would enjoy the cakes themselves.

Once Allie was settled in bed, Sam pulled out the diary. She wanted to finish it while Jackson was away. However, her thoughts were interrupted by a knock on the door. She saw the familiar Land-Rover parked out in the road and welcomed Will into the little room.

'I got your message. I thought I'd

drop by to give my acceptance to the invitation.'

'Good. Allie will be delighted.'

'And Sam? Will she be delighted too?'

She smiled and nodded, inviting him to sit down. He offered to pick her up from work the following day so that she could collect her new van.

'You heard about that, did you?'

'No-one could arrange all that without my knowing. Mrs Roberts is my staunchest ally. Tells me everything. So, what do you think of the mighty Mr Clark? I gather you're now on the payroll.'

'Not exactly. But I'm going to do some research in my spare time.'

'I'll pick you up just after one, if that's OK. And thanks again for the invite.' He hesitated as if there was something more he wanted to say but then turned to the door with a quick goodnight.

Sam settled back to her reading. It was heady stuff. She learned that Marguerite and Henry had actually kissed for the first time, near the crystal cave. She made notes of each garden feature mentioned in this deeply personal story of the forbidden lovers.

She felt a lump in her throat. This was somehow much more poignant than any of today's romantic novels. This was reality. What had happened to these young people? Their innocence was touching and belonged to a different age entirely.

Marguerite's account of the winter festivities fascinated her. The traditions of a wealthy family, from the giant Yule log being dragged in on Christmas Eve right through Christmas and the New Year. She could see how very different were the lives of the rich and their workers.

Sam yawned. It had been quite a day and despite wanting to continue reading, she was feeling sleepy. She flicked through the remaining pages. She was about halfway through the book. The final entry caught her eye and she couldn't resist reading on.

'It does not matter what happens to me now. I am disgraced and my family are to send me away forever. Without my beloved Henry, I have nothing more to live for. My child was taken away at birth.

I always knew that Henry would prove he was as good as any man. In those awful battles every man became equal. Rich or poor, losing a loved one is just as dreadful. His country took him from me.

Now it is time for me to leave. I shall hide this book amongst the many hundreds in the library and one day the right person may take time to read it. I do not believe there can ever be a greater loss than I now have to endure.

Marguerite Westcott. Cornwall.
September, 1916.'

Samantha Rayner, woman of the twenty-first century, felt tears rolling down her cheeks. She wished that she hadn't skipped to that last page. Though she had known that all of these people were long dead, the poignancy was almost too much. She was trying to discover more about the garden that filled their lives . . . wasn't she?

* * *

Lucinda was delighted when Will arrived to call for Sam the next day. In Lucinda's book, Will Heston was the man for Sam, and he would make a wonderful father for Allie.

'Ready?' Will asked. To Lucinda, he added, 'I guess she's told you all about the new van he's bought for her?'

'She mentioned something,' Lucinda conceded. 'I expect she has good reason to accept it.'

'Would you two mind not talking about me as if I'm not here? I'm ready — let's go.'

A yellow van was parked outside the Hall.

'Is that it?' Sam asked breathlessly. 'For me? But it's brand new! I was expecting something cheap and second-hand.'

'Our boss never does things by half. Mrs Roberts has some documents for you. I'll see you later. Is Jenny invited to tea, by the way?'

'You don't seriously need to ask, do you? I don't think Allie would speak to either of us again if you left Jenny behind.'

Mrs Roberts gave her a folder and a set of keys. To Sam's surprise, everything was in her own name. She had expected to see some company name there. What was she getting into? It felt a little like a trap closing around her.

Only moments later, she was driving into the village. She couldn't resist stopping at the shop to show her new toy to Lucinda.

When Allie came home from school, she merely glanced at the van standing outside the cottage and Sam felt disappointed.

'Didn't you notice anything new?' she asked.

'It's very bright. What time are Jenny and Will coming round?' Allie demanded. 'Can I have a biscuit anyway? I'm starving.'

Nothing much changes for Allie, Sam thought with a smile.

The evening with Will was a great success. They played Scrabble after tea and ended in great fits of laughter at some of the silly suggestions he was making to use up his letters. Allie challenged everything and gained a great many points. After she had gone to bed, amidst vehement protests, Sam determined to discover more about this quiet man.

'You're very good with Allie. Have you ever had children yourself?'

A spasm of anguish crossed his face. 'I don't like talking about my past, Sam. I believe in the present and the future.'

'But surely everyone's past makes them what they are now?'

He avoided the question completely. 'Tell me how you got Jackson Clark so interested in restoring this garden. Have you any idea what you're getting into?'

She stared at him. Talk about a swift change of subject! Nevertheless, she was intrigued. She knew he was a local and that his parents had died some time ago. He had disappeared from the area for abut eight years before coming back to work at Pengelly Hall. What had he been doing during those years? What sort of drama had made him want to forget his past?

He left soon after eleven, once Sam had collected Jenny from Allie's bed where she had been lying curled up behind her daughter's knees. She must have sneaked up to the little room while they were talking. Allie would have liked that.

'Be careful, Sam,' Will said earnestly. 'Jackson Clark could eat someone like you for breakfast. Make certain you know what you're doing before you sign contracts. He isn't to be trusted, believe me.' He was holding her arms as he spoke, his usually pleasant face bearing a serious expression.

'I've become very fond of you, both of you, over the past few weeks,' he went on. 'I'm not asking for anything more than your occasional company at present. But we could be working closely.' She opened her mouth to speak but he placed a warning finger on her lips. 'Now, I must go.' He planted an almost brotherly kiss on her forehead. 'Thanks for a lovely evening. Think about what I said. That man isn't to be trusted.'

Why was Will so negative about Jackson, she wondered. Maybe it was just jealousy. Perhaps his professional pride was hurt.

* * *

There were several calls each day from Jackson. He was proving impatient, always wanting things to be happening. Every spare moment she had, Sam spent at Pengelly Hall. If the weather was fine, she was poking around in the garden. Whenever possible Will joined her, hacking away the dense growth. They had bonfires most days to get rid of mountains of rubbish. They worked companionably, neither feeling the need to make conversation.

Allie was home from school for the holidays and most days was happy to potter around the grounds, playing with Jenny and taking her for walks.

On a couple of occasions, it was too wet to do much outside work and on these days Sam spent her time rummaging around in old boxes of junk. She found one or two treasures among the rubbish, including lists with the names of the estate workers from several of the surrounding villages.

She visited local churches and read war memorial tablets where there were familiar names. So many had gone to war and lost their lives. She felt a lump in her throat when she read of Henry Cobb, missing in action, Verdun 1916.

Poor young man. Maybe there would be some people still living locally, relations of those lost men.

She glanced at the flower and cleaning rotas, and, amazingly, spotted a Mrs Cobb.

When she returned home, there were two packages waiting for her. The first contained large prints of the pictures taken from the helicopter. The second parcel held a collection of maps, large-scale ordinance survey maps. They showed the main tracks around the estate and all the buildings.

Excitedly she phoned Will to see if he would come to look at them. Unexpectedly he declined, saying he was busy for the evening. She would have to work alone.

Once Allie was in bed, Sam worked on the plans. She made a sketch of the area, using the maps and pictures as guides. She had several days before Jackson's return, time to do a bit more searching and probing.

Mother and daughter set out early

the next morning, preparing to spend the whole day at the hall. She wanted to finish mapping the layout so that a strategy was ready for Jackson's return.

Will joined them and scanned the diagrams she had made.

'There must have been paths everywhere,' she mused.

'Along this way,' Will pointed. 'Let's try probing the ground and see if there's something solid underneath.' They walked along pushing metal poles into the ground.

'There's something solid here,' Allie yelled in excitement. Jenny yapped her delight and began digging the ground with her paws. 'Good girl, Jenny. Go on, dig like crazy.'

Will and Sam laughed at the animal, such a tiny animal in so great an area of wilderness.

'It'll take a bit more than you, little dog,' Will laughed.

He bent to examine what they had found, then pulled out some secateurs from his pocket and cut away a few of the brambles. With his fork he heaved away a load of foliage and there beneath were definite signs of a path. He dragged piles of dead wood and branches to one side and gradually they rolled away the debris, rather like taking up a carpet.

Once started, the mass came away easily, the root systems being very shallow over the pathways. Allie and Jenny tugged at twigs and anything else they could grab hold of, sitting down sharply several times as roots snapped suddenly. At one point, they all sat down together, practically falling on top of each other. When they pulled themselves up, they became aware of a figure standing some distance away. Jackson Clark had returned.

'You look as if you're having fun,' he called as he approached. 'Are you actually trying to prove something?'

'We didn't expect you back for a few days. Look ... we've uncovered the start of the pathway system.' Sam smiled uncertainly. This was the first time she had seen both men together.

'Jenny's helping too,' piped Allie, a little shy of the man who had so much money that he practically owned a helicopter.

'Glad to hear it. Well, I'd better leave you to it. Come over to the kitchen for lunch. We can discuss the project.'

'We've got a picnic,' Allie said defensively.

'Bring it along. The more the merrier. Mrs R. will be sure to produce something to make enough of a spread for all of us.'

'We've got Marmite sandwiches,' Allie added. 'But I s'pect you can have some of them. Mum always makes plenty.'

A flicker of a grimace passed over Jackson's handsome features.

'Thank you, Allie. I don't think I've eaten anything like that since I was at school.'

Sam found herself trying not to laugh.

'I hope you're taking plenty of

photographs of everything you're doing?' he went on. 'We must keep a record of every stage. It could be an important part of the whole project. And videos. Make video recordings of everything. Who knows, we may get a book and even a TV series out of this. I've been speaking to some people I know.'

He stood watching for a moment. If Sam had but known it, he was trying to overcome an overwhelming feeling of envy. Will, Sam, Allie and the dog looked so like a happy family.

'TV — books — he's certainly covering all the angles,' Will said once the other man had moved away.

'I'll have to organise a camera,' Sam remarked.

'Doubtless he'll provide you with state-of-the-art technology. Go for it, Sam. Get as much as you can. And hold out for a decent salary. Believe me, you'll earn every penny.'

'What is it with you? Why are you so hostile to him?'

'You don't want to know,' he snapped. 'Now, shall we go and see what delights he's organised for lunch? I doubt your Marmite sandwiches will feature too highly in the feast.'

'Lovely to see you all,' Mrs Roberts called as she welcomed them in. 'The bathroom's through there.'

'I hope it's all right, us all descending on you like this. I've got a few boring sandwiches,' Sam offered and looked at the lunch she had prepared in admiration. 'How on earth can you produce this spread at a moment's notice? Amazing!'

'Organisation, a well-stocked freezer and a microwave set to defrost. It all took a bit of getting used to, this new-fangled technology, but I couldn't manage without it now.'

Jackson appeared, a folder bulging with papers under his arm.

'Help yourselves. Fine spread, Mrs Roberts. Thank you.'

They each filled a plate with fresh rolls and salads. There were several different cooked meats, cheese, hard-boiled eggs and a large pork pie. Very deliberately Allie took two of the Marmite sandwiches, smiling at Sam as she did so.

They took their plates outside to eat in the warm sunshine. Jackson provided a bottle of deliciously cold white wine, and lemonade for Allie.

'What have you been doing while I was away?' he asked.

Sam listed the various activities, showed him her diagrams, and mentioned the information she had gleaned from the local churches.

'Excellent. I see I've got myself a very conscientious researcher.'

'I hope you appreciate just how much she has done,' Will said rather stiffly.

'I certainly do, and I've made plans. We'll discuss it later, though. Now, what's our next move, Samantha?'

She didn't miss the look of surprise that flashed across Will's face. He didn't like the fact that Jackson seemed to have appointed her as the head of this project over himself.

Plans for the coming months were made. It was agreed that Will should oversee the general clearing work and that he should employ extra labour. He was given the go-ahead to find a second-hand digger.

'Right, if you want to get back to work, Will, I just need a few minutes more to talk to Samantha,' Jackson said, collecting up the papers strewn over the table.

Will strode off, whistling for Jenny. Jackson watched him go then glanced at Sam. 'You all seem to get on very well,' he remarked.

'Yes. Allie's deeply in love with Jenny for a start.'

'And you? How do you feel about Will?'

'I'm not sure that's any of your business.'

'Just wondering. You looked remarkably like a family, coming across the lawn earlier. Do you have plans to make that a reality?'

She said nothing and looked coldly at him.

'I see.' He shrugged. 'Well now — what are we going to do about you and your job? I really need you here full-time. Would you consider living here at the Hall? You need to be on-site, and you said your cottage is job-dependent. We'll sort out a proper wage, of course. And you'll have to learn to use the computer. We'll need a secretary in time but not yet. As to salary . . . ' He named a figure that made her gasp.

'That's very generous of you. I'm not sure I'm worth it,' she breathed.

'You'll be earning every penny of it, mark my words.'

She remembered Will's warning and sensed that he wasn't exaggerating.

'Well, what do you say?' Jackson asked, staring intently at her.

'Can I think about it? I'd like to discuss it with Allie.'

'OK. But don't keep me waiting. I'm not renowned for my patience.'

The hard work of clearing the paths kept her occupied for the rest of the day. By the time they had finished, they had a small mountain of rubbish and almost fifty yards of exposed path.

'My back will never be the same again,' Sam groaned. 'I need a long soak in a hot bath with every herbal remedy known to mankind.'

'After that, how about I take you and Allie out for something to eat?' Will suggested.

'If Allie agrees, thanks. That would be nice.'

Will smiled happily. If his little dog was involved, Allie was a pushover.

Sam told her daughter of Jackson's proposals.

'Sounds cool to me,' was the verdict.

★ ★ ★

'We're coming to live next door to you,' Allie blurted out when Will collected them. 'Mr Clark's giving Mum and me an apartment. I'll be able to play with

Jenny every day.'

Will's jaw tightened. He looked at Sam, his eyebrows raised.

'*Might*, Allie. I have a couple of days to think it over,' Sam put in.

He glanced at Allie, sitting with Jenny on her knee in the back of his Land-Rover. Sam nodded. It could wait.

'I'm starving, despite that lovely lunch. How about you, Allie?' she asked.

'Can I have scampi and chips with special sauce, if they've got it?'

The meal passed with as much fun as they always had when they were together, and it was almost Allie's bedtime by the time they got back.

By the time she had tucked Allie into bed, Will was spooning coffee into two mugs. 'I hope you don't mind,' he said. 'I thought you might want to discuss a few things.'

'I want to know why you're so suspicious of Jackson,' she said at once.

He shrugged. 'I don't want you to be

used. He picks people up and drops them when he's taken what he wants. You'd be stuck without a home and a job. I don't want to see you hurt.'

There was obviously something personal in his reaction, Sam thought. Something from his past? Could Will have known Jackson before he'd bought Pengelly?

'I'm taking up Jackson's offer,' she told Will the next morning. 'I can't let this chance slip by. I owe it to Allie. I'll be earning an excellent salary. And if it does all fall around my ears, so be it. I've managed before and I'll manage again.'

'Then I guess that makes my idea of offering you rooms at the lodge redundant,' he said quietly.

She stared at him. 'What do you mean?'

'I've been re-decorating a room for Allie. That's what I was doing the other night when you phoned. I wanted to surprise you. No strings, of course.'

Sam stared at him. Move in with

Will? It was out of the question.

'I knew you needed to be nearer the Hall but I had no idea that man would come up with a more attractive proposition,' he explained. 'I could offer you a home and it would have been nice for Allie to have Jenny to play with.'

Sam smiled tremulously. 'You are a dear, sweet man and I'm very touched. Thank you so much. But you must know I couldn't.' As she reached up and kissed his cheek, he put out his arms to enfold her but then thought better of it.

'I don't give up easily, mind,' he added with a grimace.

A Battle Of Wills

'I've decided, Jackson,' she told Jackson Clark when she saw him later.

He nodded. 'Good. When can you move in?'

'How do you know which way my decision went?'

He gave a knowing grin. 'There was never any doubt. I make offers that can't be refused. There's a place you can have right away. I'll show you round immediately.' He led the way along the corridor from his office and used a key to open a door.

'This has two bedrooms and a decent lounge. There's a kitchen and bathroom, of course, and there's an outside entrance at the back. You'll be quite independent. If you need more space for putting up guests, just ask Mrs R. She'll arrange a room for you. Any questions?'

'I don't think so. But who's this place designed for? It's all ready for someone, that's obvious.'

'Mrs R had been working on it. She put the final touches to it while I was away. It's all yours if you like it, although you could have one of the new conversions when they're ready, if you prefer.'

'This is wonderful,' Sam muttered. 'It's beautiful. I'd love it.'

'You need have no worries about the place being secure. I won't invade your territory at any time, except by invitation. Absolutely no strings.'

'It's lovely, Jackson. May I fetch Allie to look? She'll be thrilled. She's always complaining that she hasn't got enough space where we are.'

As she went down the stairs, she almost skipped. It was fully-furnished and he had offered to change anything she wanted. It was the second offer of a home in one day. And Jackson was also the second man to specify a 'no strings' deal. Obviously he had no romantic inclinations towards her, so why was he being so nice?

The next hurdle she had to face was telling Lucinda, who was seeing to the last customers of the day when they drove up in the little yellow van.

'I'm longing for a cuppa,' Lucinda said as she closed the till. 'Pop the kettle on, will you, love? I expect you've come to tell me something important this late in the day.'

Shrewd lady, Lucinda, Sam thought. She was quick to realise things were happening.

Lucinda came slowly into the room. 'Oh, I must sit down! My poor legs are killing me. Now then, Allie, if your Mum says it's OK, you help yourself to one of those chocolate biscuits you're so fond of.' Sam nodded her agreement and the little girl went off into shop.

'So, when do you want to leave?' Lucinda asked at once. 'That is what you want to say, isn't it? It's been coming for days, hasn't it?'

'I'm sorry, Lucinda. I hate letting you

down. But yes, Jackson — Mr Clark — has offered me a job and a flat, and I'd like to take it. Imagine, Lucinda, I'm going to be in charge of re-building that wonderful garden, once planning permission and all the legal stuff's sorted. I'm so thrilled! I'll serve my month's notice, of course, and we'll move out of the cottage whenever you like. The flat is all ready at the Hall.'

'I've been doing a bit of deciding of my own,' Lucinda mused. 'I guessed something like this was coming, though I'll admit I'd hoped it was going to be Will's offer you'd accepted.'

'Will's offer? You knew about that? How? I only found out about it this morning.'

'He asked me what colours little girls like best. Doing up his old junk room, I understand.'

'I see.' Sam looked down at her tea. 'So what decisions have you been making?'

'I'm going to sell the shop and your cottage. I've had enough. It's time I

157

retired before it's too late for me to enjoy my remaining years. I'll stay in my home, of course, but your little place — well, it can go. I've had enough of owning property.'

'Oh, Lucinda, I'm so sorry. You wouldn't have done it if I hadn't let you down.'

'You aren't letting me down, lovely. As a matter of fact, I called in at the estate agent this morning. He's coming over tomorrow to give me an estimate.'

Sam laughed and hugged the old lady. 'How about I go and get some fish and chips and we'll all go back to the cottage for supper?' she suggested.

'Yeah!' shouted Allie from the shop. She had been listening to every word.

Afterwards they all walked down the hill to see Lucinda home. The sea crashed on to the beach and there was the unmistakable tang of salt and seaweed in the air.

'I'll miss being able to go down to the beach whenever I want to,' Allie said as they strolled back.

'You hardly ever go down,' Sam pointed out.

'Funny that, isn't it? When you visit the seaside, you always go walking on the beach but when you live here you hardly ever go.'

'I think that's called taking things for granted.'

'What did Lucinda mean about Will's offer?'

Sam found it difficult to explain to the girl, whose reaction was unexpected. 'That's nice of him. But the Hall is cool. It's a really neat apartment. And Clark's stinking rich. Anyway, you like him best, don't you? It wouldn't be fair to Will to pretend.'

★ ★ ★

It was another couple of weeks before Sam and Allie moved to the Hall. They had a large bedroom each with plenty of cupboard space, the lounge was also a good size and the kitchen well-equipped and modern. Once their own

159

things were added, it looked like a real home. Allie was delighted with it all, particularly the little outside staircase that led to the main entrance.

Lucinda had found someone to help in the shop and the cottage was empty with a *For Sale* sign stuck in the garden. It was the end of an era and another new beginning.

They began the new week with a whole day of meetings. Will, Jackson and Sam planned strategies and defined their new roles. Will was pacified with a new contract, putting him on a level with Sam.

Mrs Roberts kept them supplied with food and drink and made a friend for life when she suggested that Allie should spend the day with her, learning to cook properly.

There were many occasions when Sam wondered if she had taken on too much. Jackson's action list left her gasping. He had also begun his computer lessons with her, and Sam was terrified of all the hi-tech equipment, of doing something wrong and losing valuable data, but Jackson was remarkably patient.

On one occasion, she pressed a key and everything she had been working on disappeared.

'Oh no! It's swallowed everything!' she yelled. 'You horrible machine! Why don't you like me?'

'It doesn't have a mind of its own, you know. Let me see what's happened.' Jackson came over to her desk, pressed a couple of keys and, like magic, the text came back.

'You are a genius!' Sam smiled happily. 'How did you do that?'

'Magic!' He lifted her hand and placed a kiss on it.

'Thank you,' she said, not entirely sure she was talking about the work he had rescued. 'I think I'll see how the men are getting on outside,' she said. She felt she needed some fresh air.

'I'll come with you. It's good to let everyone see that we're interested in what's going on. That way, you won't be cheated,' he added as he followed her to the door.

Allie was watching the digger at work. It was a sizeable machine and capable of scooping up vast piles of weeds and debris. Will was directing proceedings.

'Right, Tom, we'll get this lot moved over and have a bonfire. You can help, Allie,' he called.

She trotted after him. Her new red wellies had already acquired a muddy, lived-in look. She gave a wave to her mum and Jackson, far too busy to stop and talk.

'Seem to be making great progress, don't they?' Sam said. 'They'll have the whole path round the edge cleared soon. I wish we could find some old maps and plans to show the actual plan of the grounds.'

'How about the County Archives? Have you tried them?' Jackson suggested.

'Good idea. I'll go and find their number.' She was off again on a new mission.

***

Sam had finally tracked down Mrs Cobb from the neighbouring parish and with an unexpected sense of anticipation she drove to the next village. Could this Mrs Cobb be some relation of the man so beloved by Marguerite Westcott? Would she be able to shed some light on what had happened to the daughter of the wealthy owners of Pengelly Hall?

The stone-built Cornish cottage stood back from the road. The garden was a riot of colour, with flowers of every kind. Sam knocked at the door and a grey-haired woman opened it, smiling her welcome. 'I'm Mrs Cobb. Do come in.'

Sam followed her into the immaculate living-room where vases of flowers picked from the garden stood on the window sills.

'What a lovely garden you have. So many different plants and colours.'

Mrs Cobb looked pleased. 'That's

my husband's work. He enjoys his garden. Now then, perhaps you'd like to sit down and tell me how you think I can help you. I'm not sure I know anything much but I'm curious.'

'You may have heard that we're restoring the gardens at Pengelly Hall?' Sam began. 'Well, I'm trying to find anyone who used to work there or who can give me information. There are very few records.'

'Well now, that's a tricky one. I believe it was quite something till the war. The First World War, of course. Then nobody wanted to work at the Hall any more. A lot of our local men did work there, as you know. Terrible times by all accounts. Nobody in this village escaped without they knew someone who'd been killed.'

'I noticed your name — or rather your husband's name, on the war memorial.'

'That'd be Henry Cobb. Suppose he would have been my husband's uncle. I think he worked on the estate. He were but a young man when he went to the war. Such a waste. They called it giving their lives for their country. Strikes me they didn't have much choice. Didn't learn much by it all, did they? Second War took another lot of them. I suppose my father-in-law was one of the lucky ones. Charles Cobb. He came back, though he didn't live to much of an age. Never got over the awful things he saw.'

'Do you know anything about Henry and the daughter of the Hall? I heard they were sweethearts.'

Mrs Cobb frowned, the smile slipped from her face and her mouth tightened. 'I don't know anything about that. Oh, there were rumours all right. It's said that the Heston family were involved, but don't ask me how. Tried to hush it up, they all did. It was rumoured that money changed hands. It's all too long ago to dig it up. Some things are best left.'

Sam was electrified. Heston. Could Will's family have some connection with Marguerite? Even Will himself?

Mrs Cobb busied herself with tea-making and called her husband from the back garden. The elderly man came in, removing his boots at the back door as instructed. He was a taciturn man, not used to company.

'This young lady is trying to find out about the men and women who used to work up at the Hall in its heyday,' his wife informed him.

'Dunno why she should bother. They've all been dead for years.'

Sam tried to explain what she wanted and why, but he stared silently into his tea-cup.

'Where's my mug?' he asked. 'Tea don't taste the same from these silly little cups.' Evidently his contribution to the interview was over.

'Can you give me any names I could contact?' Sam asked as she was eventually shown to the door.

'Will Heston do still work at the Hall, don't he? Can't he help? I'll have a bit of a think and I'll telephone if I comes up with anything. Is that Emily Roberts still working there? She might give you a few names.'

'Thanks so much. Keep in touch and I'm grateful for your help.

* * *

Will's bonfire was still blazing when she returned.

'How's it going?' she called.

'Great fun. Always enjoyed a good blaze. How's life in the office?'

'Better since I escaped!'

'Fancy a drink tonight? Mrs R. will listen out for Allie. I asked her earlier.'

'I'd planned a quiet evening,' she protested, but finally she was persuaded.

'Will's really great, isn't he, Mum?' Allie said when she returned for tea. 'I'm glad you're going out with him tonight. He needs a break. So do you. You've been working like crazy since we moved in here. I'm really having fun. I'm so glad we moved here. It's great!'

'You'll be back at school soon. I might have to drive you, or maybe the bus will come and pick you up.'

Allie suddenly looked stricken. 'I'd forgotten about school! So I really have to go? It would be just as good for me if I stayed here and helped. You could teach me all about computing and Will can teach me gardening. Mrs Roberts is already teaching me to cook. There's not much else I need to know.'

'Nice try, Allie, but school is compulsory. You're going back next week, so make the most of it.'

Later in the local pub, Sam recounted Allie's theory of education to Will. He laughed. 'I'm afraid my teaching days are over. She's such a great kid — and you're a great lady. I haven't given up on you yet, you know.' His face became unusually serious. 'One day . . . I'll sweep you off your feet. I mean to marry you, Sam.'

She looked at him in surprise. She hadn't dreamed he could be so candid about his feelings. 'Oh, Will,' she said softly, 'I thought we'd agreed. We can't work together with this sort of talk still in the background. I . . . I can't love you in that way.'

'Oh, so does that mean you could love me in some other sort of way?'

Many of her feelings stemmed from gratitude to him for being a friend to both her and Allie. She realised she thought of him in much the same way as she did her brother.

'Perhaps you remind me of my brother,' she admitted.

'Oh, well, thanks! But I can assure you none of my feelings are at all fraternal.' His expression was crestfallen for a moment. Then he shrugged. 'You'll come round. Eventually.'

'I don't want to hurt you. I guess I'm not the marrying kind. Not again. I daren't risk it.'

'So you had one failed marriage. Didn't we all? But for Allie's sake, please consider my offer.'

'You were married before?' she asked.

'Yes.'

'What happened?' she probed, but his face remained impassive, a shutter clamping down to hide the expression in his eyes. 'We can't have a relationship if we can't be honest with each other,' she pressed.

'It was a stupid idea. How could I ever interest someone like you? Especially not with such competition. But Jackson Clark's no good for you, Sam. Don't let yourself fall in love with him. I know what he's like. Now, do you want another drink?' When she shook her head, he stood up. 'Excuse me, I think I'll have a re-fill myself.'

She was speechless. What did he really know about Jackson Clark?

He came back with a fixed smile on his face. 'I see there's a regatta in the village next weekend. There's a poster behind the bar. They usually have a few silly things . . . raft races, fancy dress, that sort of thing. Allie would love it.'

'Sounds like fun,' she agreed, relieved to be back on safer ground.

Will drove her back to the Hall and

leaned over to kiss her cheek as she was getting out of the car.

'Just a *brotherly* peck,' he teased. 'Night, Sam.'

She was surprised to see Jackson standing outside his office.

'Have a nice evening?' he asked, with a hint of displeasure.

'Yes, thanks. You?'

'I was bored.'

'I'm sorry. You should have come out for a drink with us.'

'I'm hardly going to play gooseberry, am I?'

'Will and I are just friends.'

'You seem pretty affectionate for friends. Just how much do you know about him? He's a good worker, which is why I employ him, but he doesn't say much.'

'So what? Most people like to keep things private. You don't say much about yourself either.'

'Fair enough. I'll say goodnight.' He turned and went into the office.

She felt he had been hinting that he

knew something about Will, and after tossing around, unable to sleep, she decided to read more of Marguerite's diary.

She flicked through the pages. Always written without any dates, she could only guess at the period. The daily lives of the family were detailed and seemed to be a long saga of small events. Tea taken with this or that person; the arrival of one of the first cars in the area; visitors from up-country.

For Sam, the most interesting parts were the accounts of Marguerite's meeting with Henry. They always took place in the garden and their favourite places were yet to be discovered. She could imagine the ghosts of the young lovers, haunting the grotto, or crystal cave as the girl called it.

★　★　★

'What exactly is there between you and Will Heston?' Jackson asked over coffee the next morning.

172

'You've asked me that before.'

'I don't believe you gave me a reply.'

'I'm not sure that it has anything to do with you.'

'Maybe I'd like it to be.' He hated talking about personal matters but he felt forced to say something. He was jealous of Will. He wanted to spend time relaxing with Samantha. Take her out, wine and dine her. She was so different from most of the career-minded women he met. But he wanted to get her away from the Hall and her preoccupation with the wretched garden. He would be forty in a couple of years. He had a fortune to show for his life's work, but his private life was empty.

'Will you have dinner with me tonight?' he asked suddenly.

'I . . . I'm not sure. Is it business?'

'No, this time it's pleasure. I'd like to get to know you better. In here, it's all work. I want to know more about Samantha, the person.'

'Mrs Roberts will be tired of cooking

for us,' she hedged, searching for an excuse.

'I was thinking we'd go out somewhere. Somewhere very expensive. Mrs R. will listen for Allie, won't she?'

'She looked after her last night. It doesn't seem fair,' she protested.

'No problem. Leave it with me.' Jackson went out of the office and Sam settled back to work, this time with a smile on her face. But what would she wear? Now she had enough money to replenish her wardrobe, she never had time to go shopping. Maybe she and Allie could go together . . .

The perfect chance arrived when the County Archivist telephoned. He had located some old documents, including maps and plans. She could come and collect copies at any time.

'No time like the present,' she told him. 'I'll be with you in an hour or so.'

She would drive to Truro with Allie, and once they had the documents they would go shopping. She rushed to tell Mrs Roberts of her plans.

'Mr Jackson says you'd like me to sit for you again tonight. Your room's as good as mine.'

'Thanks, I really appreciate it. Do you know where Allie is? I thought I'd take the chance to stock up on school things. She needs shoes and, oh, everything.'

She went off to find her and a few minutes later they were driving to Truro.

'This is all a bit sudden,' Allie complained. 'I was just going to give Jenny a bath. She rolled in a pile of ash from the bonfires. She's black even on her white bits. Will said I could.'

Soon mother and daughter were enjoying the rare treat of shopping. It was a long time since Sam had had enough money to indulge. Allie had always had the things she needed, thanks to Martin's allowance, but there had been nothing left for fun things.

They soon collected quite a pile of colourful carrier bags.

'This is great, Mum!' Allie chirped.

'What are we going to get for you now? Let's sort you out.'

As she dived off to burrow into racks of inappropriate dresses and skirts, Sam smiled. She wasn't going to be told by a nine-year-old what she should wear! She found a long, dark red dress which she adored on sight. It was a perfect fit, too.

'Can I have a CD player, Mum? I'd like to listen to the music everyone else listens to, not your boring old stuff. Please, Mum?'

'It's your birthday soon. You might have one then.'

'Was my dad anything like Will?' the girl asked on the drive home.

'Not really. Why do you ask?'

'I just wondered. He's very nice though. And Jenny's brilliant. He's nuts about you, that's obvious. And he likes me quite a lot.'

'Oh, Allie, you are funny. He isn't nuts about me, as you put it. Besides, there's a big difference between liking someone because they're nice and deciding to get married.'

'Might you think about getting married, though?'

'Not really, no. What would you think if I did?'

'I'd think, 'about time too.' but not just because of Jenny. Will likes us both and he's very good with me, you said so yourself. Do you think he might have been a dad sometime? Else why is he so good with children?'

'I don't know — he won't talk about the past. Says the present and future are what's important. Maybe he's right.'

'P'raps he was a teacher or something.'

Sam gave a start as the word struck a chord. What exactly had he said last night? Something about his teaching days being over?

'You could be right,' she agreed slowly.

'Where've you been all this time?' Will asked when they drove back into the grounds. 'I was worried.'

'Shopping,' Allie said happily. 'We've

both got loads of new clothes and things and now Mum can go out to posh places.'

'Glad to hear it,' Will said with a grin. 'Maybe I should take you both out somewhere posh.'

'She's going out with Mr Clark to somewhere posh tonight, aren't you, Mum?'

'Well yes, I suppose so,' she admitted.

Will's face looked thunderous. 'Don't you ever listen?' he hissed. She might as well have announced that she was about to sell herself into the white-slave trade!

'No-one tells me what I should or shouldn't do, Will.'

He turned and stomped away angrily.

Allie looked anxious. 'Shouldn't I have told him about you going out with Mr Clark?'

'Forget it, Allie, it wasn't a secret. He's just upset. Let's get the van unpacked and fill up our wardrobes.'

'It's a good job we moved,' mused Allie. 'There wouldn't have been room for all this in the cottage. Good old Mr

Clark. Even if he's not as nice as Will, the money makes up for it, doesn't it?'

'You're becoming too mercenary for your own good, young lady.'

'I don't know what that means,' Allie replied. 'But you must admit, there's more going on here than in Hertfordshire.'

Warnings About Each Other

'You are enjoying your work, aren't you, Samantha?' Jackson asked as they reached dessert.

'Of course. It's everything I could have dreamed of.'

'And you do have everything you need in the apartment? And Allie — is there anything she needs?'

'Apart from a dog and a CD player? No, she's fine. But thanks for asking.'

'Maybe she needs a computer for school work?'

'Certainly not. But it's a kind thought.'

He gave a slight shrug.

'You really do look very beautiful tonight. New outfit? Sorry, perhaps you don't like personal comments.'

'Jackson . . . thank you. But what is it you really want to say? I can't help feeling you're making small talk and that isn't like you. Usually it's straight to the point.'

'I know. I'm not very good at being subtle. Not enough practice. I wanted to get to know you better.' He paused. 'All right. The plain truth is, I don't like to see you wasting your time on someone like Will Heston. Don't get me wrong but he has a cupboard full of skeletons. He's not to be trusted. I don't want you to be let down.'

He made almost the same comments about you, Mr Jackson Clark, she thought.

'What do you know about his background?' she asked.

'Will was a teacher. It's on his CV. He said he gave up so that he could return to Cornwall and that he preferred gardening to dealing with young people.'

'I suspected he might have been a teacher. And do you know the real reason he gave up?'

'I accept what he says. But I do know he left a wife and young child when he came to Cornwall. My . . . well, a relation of mine knew him at one time. There was some scandal, but as it wasn't proved, I never followed it up. It would have been privileged information in any case, and not relevant to the work he's doing now. The wife and child disappeared. That's it, really. A few facts and a lot of supposition. Just don't get yourself into anything you can't handle.'

'It didn't stop you giving him a job,' she pointed out.

'He was already here when I bought the place. I inherited him. But I had no reason to doubt his abilities. He's a good worker. His personal life is his own affair.'

'Thanks for telling me.'

He shrugged. 'Well, I hope you don't mind my directness. If there is something I want, I make sure I get it, one way or another. Now, coffee?'

As he called the waiter, Sam contemplated his words. Why were these two men warning her off each other?

* * *

It was with a thrill that Sam opened the Archivist's file next morning. It was everything she had been hoping for. There were scale drawings and a complete layout of the grounds.

She made notes and scribbled comments to follow up later. She and Will could walk over much of this land and see exactly what they were looking for.

'I hope you realise this is going to cost an absolute fortune, she warned Jackson when he came in and looked over her shoulder. 'Even the minimum work will be phenomenal. How are we going to manage it?' she asked.

'We should be eligible for grants. And if we plan to open to the public, we need planning permission. That's the next step. We need provision for things like car parking and toilets. A shop and plant sales, eventually. I'll get my chap down from London. He'll sort it all out for us. Don't hire anyone just yet.'

'I wouldn't dream of it. But maybe we should start with something small. If the gardens closest to the house are made usable, it should help make the apartments more attractive. I've just seen the brochure. They're not exactly cheap, are they?'

'Certainly not. I think you're right, though.'

'I'll leave you to your calls and walk the land with Will. I can start to look properly for the various features like the other summer-house. I may even locate the elusive sundial.'

'Which is where I came in. Would you mind if I came too? I want to be a part of this discovery. I can always claim to be the official photographer.'

She made photocopies of the sheets while he called his architect friend, then, picking up a clipboard and maps for each of them, they went out into the warm sun.

'I must say, we've been lucky with the weather these last few weeks. Hang on — I'll just get a shot of you with your clipboard, looking industrious. Smile, please.' He clicked away with the expensive camera looking relaxed and almost boyish in his enthusiasm.

They found Will, Allie and Jenny and carried on to the walled areas behind the house.

'According to the various diagrams and pictures, there are three or maybe even four walled gardens. One, we know, is an exotic fruit area . . . peaches, apricots, pineapples and so on. We have the ruins of the greenhouses in there. Next is what must have been a vegetable garden, and then a flower garden, presumably with the sundial standing in it. Let's try to get through that door at the back. Everyone feeling strong?'

However, the hinges were rotten and the door gave way easily. Through the gap, they could see another expanse of weeds, tangles of brambles, trails of ivy and giant cow-parsley heads. Nettles added their bite and the hum of bees and fluttering butterflies gave a sense of a busy life still going on despite the canopy of weeds. They pushed their way through and Jenny gave a sudden yelp as she disappeared from sight.

'She's fallen down a great big hole!' yelled Allie.

They crossed to the spot where the dog had disappeared and found a circular hole, brick-edged, carefully constructed in the centre of the garden. Sam pulled out the diagram again.

'This must be the dipping pond, where they collected water for the hot-houses. We're exactly here.' She jabbed a finger into the middle of one of the walled areas. 'That means the sundial garden must be in the next space.' She turned the map around to get the direction correct and pointed at a well-covered piece of wall at one side. Meanwhile Jenny had been hauled from the hole which turned out to be only three feet deep.

'Good job she found it first or we'd have fallen in ourselves,' Allie said excitedly. 'This is fun, like following a treasure map. Three paces left and dig down for two feet.'

Jackson was still busy with his camera, taking pictures of everything, even the hole where Jenny had disappeared.

Holding Will's hand, Allie wandered off, chatting nineteen to the dozen.

'They get on well, don't they?' remarked Jackson.

'Yes,' smiled Sam. 'Must be the teacher in him.'

She looked up as Jackson took yet another picture of her. 'I hate pictures of me. They prove how awful I look most of the time.'

'I think you look fine.'

'Come over here,' called Will. 'The Italian garden is just on the other side of this wall. There are piles of rubble here. I can still see the remains of the walls.'

Sam consulted her maps and diagrams. 'It says that this is the site of the bothy. What's a bothy? Will? Some Cornish jargon?' she asked.

'I think it was accommodation for the gardener's boys. I'll look it up. Anyway, if that's what it is, we've found it.'

'Let's start to clear that area and get it back to how it used to look. It'll be so exciting. It'll be a good project to start with. What do you say?' Sam's enthusiasm was infectious.

'Good thinking. But don't underestimate the scale and cost of it. The summer house will have to be re-built from scratch and the ornamental pond will need digging out and probably re-lining,' Will warned.

'Let's go round and take a proper look,' Sam said.

They fought their way in through the blocked gateway. Impulsively Sam began tugging at the weeds growing in the pond, but the whole thing was filled with silt and a mass of root structures that defied any tug she could give it. Will went off to collect some tools.

'I hope we can do this,' Sam said, anxiously biting her lip.

'You needn't look so worried. I've every confidence that you can achieve anything you want.' Jackson grinned, suddenly looking years younger. 'Right. Give me your orders.'

Sam smiled back at him. 'Most of the plants will have to go. They're too leggy and old to recover.'

'It feels like this is the real start of the creation,' Jackson announced.

'There's a lot of destruction before the re-creation begins,' Sam said ruefully. 'Are you dressed for this?' she added, looking at his designer jeans and trainers.

He shrugged carelessly. 'They're only clothes.'

Will returned with a wheelbarrow stacked high with tools and several pairs of gardening gloves and a mean-looking chainsaw. They hacked at the hedges, pulled out weeds and made an enormous pile of debris ready for burning. It felt good to see the bare ground beginning to appear.

'I like this place,' Allie squeaked

excitedly. 'You get plenty of bonfires. When's lunch? I'm starving!'

As one, the adults looked at their watches and exclaimed.

'Good grief, it's almost two! Mrs R. will think I've got lost,' Jackson said. 'I'll see what she can organise.'

He returned a few minutes later. Mrs Roberts was preparing a picnic.

'This soil is pretty well burnt out,' Sam said poking around.

'What does that mean?' Jackson asked.

'Several tons of decent topsoil and compost,' Will answered.

'Make a list of everything and I'll get it ordered. We need a plan of the shrubs and herbaceous plants we'll be using. Samantha, that's your task.'

As expected, the housekeeper had provided her usual feast. Seemingly in seconds, she had conjured up Cornish pasties, fresh tomatoes and crisp lettuce.

'How on earth do you do it?' Sam marvelled.

'I told you, dear — the freezer and the microwave. I bake when no-one's around and it all goes in the freezer. Now, there're peaches and apples for dessert. My heavens, what a mess! I thought you were building something, not destroying it.'

'Like the Phoenix, Mrs R., it will grow from the ashes,' Jackson said as if believing it for the first time.

He hadn't enjoyed himself so much in his entire life. He was going to be a part of this re-birth from the soil upwards. No more working in the office all the time. He wanted hands-on experience. Soon, it would be time to bring his brother Dominic to join them. Once that happened, everything he had been working so hard for all his life would finally be achieved.

★　★　★

It was a happy day at the village regatta and raft races. Watching Will and her daughter together, Sam realised that

191

they seemed to be getting more like a family every day. It was strange feeling, especially as she found herself thinking of Jackson far more than she should. It was almost the reverse of Marguerite, wealthy daughter of the house falling in love with the humble gardener. But the wealthy owner of all this could never harbour any feelings for her, the humble gardener.

When the day was over, Will came back to the Hall with them and saw their apartment for the first time.

'Very grand,' he commented. 'Much grander than anything I could have provided. You've done all right for yourself, Mrs Rayner. Now, who fancies fish and chips for supper? I'll go and fetch some once I've fed Jenny.'

'Can I come?' called Allie from her room.

'OK.'

While she waited for them to return, Sam read some more of the diary. She was still bewildered about the location of some of the places Marguerite described. Interestingly, the bothy was mentioned.

'*I am shocked by the conditions imposed on the poor boys who work in our garden. It is primitive and they have only straw and thin blankets to sleep. It can't be pleasant to have to shovel the evil-smelling stuff that makes the pineapple house work. Henry explained it to me when I asked how he managed to sleep in the bothy. What they are forced to do, just to provide us with pineapples! I expect few of them have ever even tasted a pineapple.*'

Precious information, Sam thought. So, there had been a pineapple house and the bothy had indeed been some sort of dwelling for the gardener's boys. The evil-smelling stuff must have been manure, the heat from it being used to force the fruit. She had read about the practise somewhere in one of her father's books.

It was another piece of information to fit into the jigsaw, and she could hardly wait to tell Will and Jackson of her discoveries. But she had to find some other way to pass on the information to them for she wasn't yet prepared to share her precious diary with anyone.

They sat on the floor and ate the fish and chips out of the paper.

'They taste much nicer like this, don't they?' Allie said.

'And best of all,' Sam added, 'there's no washing-up!'

Once Allie was in bed, Sam decided to ask Will about his family. She poured them each a glass of wine and drew in a deep breath. She must be careful or he would close up the way he usually did.

'Have your family always lived around this village?'

'I think so. I don't know anything beyond my grandparents. Though I never really knew them, either. My grandfather died when I was just a kid. My gran lived for fifteen more years.'

'Do you know his name?'

'Why would you want to know that?'

'Research. I'm trying to trace people who may have worked on the estate.'

He gave a shrug. It was harmless enough and at least she had stopped questioning him about his own past, the part of his life he truly wanted to forget.

'I think it may have been Henry or Harry.'

Sam's eyes gleamed. Suppose Marguerite's child hadn't died at all? The money that had changed hands, according to Mrs Cobb, could have been payment for the Hestons to adopt Marguerite's baby. She would have named the child Henry, after its father, and the name had passed on down. If that really was the case, Will could be Marguerite's own great-grandson.

'When did your grandfather die?'

'In nineteen-sixty-something — sixty-five or six. He was quite young, so they all said. Only fifty. My own father died when he was around fifty, too.'

Her mind raced through a series of calculations. If Will's grandfather had died around nineteen-sixty-five, aged fifty, he was the right age to have been Marguerite's son. She sensed that she might have stumbled on a truth that not even Will's own parents had known.

★   ★   ★

Jackson's reply to her inquiry about a nice weekend was almost as evasive as one of Will's replies. Wherever he had been, he wasn't going to talk about it.

'I found out more about the bothy,' she told him. Once more she passed on the facts without revealing the source of her information. The story of the young girl was too private. She pulled out the old photograph, taken in the Italian garden, and together they stared at it. The rear of the bothy was apparent behind the little summer house.

'What's the next move?' Jackson asked.

'We burned more rubbish this morning. Now I'd like to get a digger in there to clear out all the spent soil and the pond. Then we can start rebuilding the summer-house and the pond itself. Could you spare one of the bricklayers from the house? To sort through the bricks we can re-use?'

'We ought to get someone signed on for a few weeks. There'll be plenty to do. My architect is coming down this week so we need to show him exactly what we want to do. Clear yourself from Wednesday onwards.'

★   ★   ★

'I'll miss you when you go back to school tomorrow,' Sam told Allie, 'I'll come and pick you up, of course, and we'll ask if the bus comes this way. It's been an eventful holiday, hasn't it?'

'If I hadn't wanted to walk along the cliff in the first place, we might never have found this place at all. It's all thanks to me.'

'Yes, Allie, you're probably right.'

After they had finished tea that evening, Will arrived, carrying a package which he solemnly handed to Allie. 'This is a present, from Jenny and me, to say thank you for looking after her so well all through the holidays.'

Allie blushed with pleasure. 'Thanks, Will. But you didn't need to buy me anything. I was really happy to have Jenny around.' She pulled away the wrapping paper and gave a shriek of joy. 'It's a CD player. Look, Mum! Just what I wanted.'

'The CDs are from Jenny,' he added. 'She thought you'd like some Bach and the Jack Russell of Spring . . . and . . . '

Allie shrieked with laughter. 'You are silly, Will! Thanks ever so much.' She flung her arms round his neck. 'You're the kindest ever person in the whole world. Isn't he, Mum?'

Sam was standing watching, not knowing quite how she felt. She had been planning to give Allie a CD player herself for her birthday.

'You're a very lucky girl. You can listen for a while in bed.'

Allie gave them both a hug and a kiss, and with calls of thanks she bounded off.

'That really was kind of you, Will, but you shouldn't. She's had a wonderful summer and she's adored playing with Jenny.'

'I wanted an excuse. And don't worry, it wasn't expensive.'

'How did you know it was what she wanted?'

'She . . . er . . . mentioned it. But she wasn't hinting. She just talked about 'when she got one for her birthday'. You'll think of something else?'

'No doubt.'

'Actually, there is one other thing I know she would like, but I definitely need to ask you first. Jenny's having pups. She got out one night when she shouldn't, so heaven knows what they'll be like. I haven't said anything to Allie, of course, but they're due in a few weeks. I reckon they'll be ready to go just in nice time for her birthday.'

'I see. I'll have to ask Jackson. I'm not sure how he'd feel about a dog sharing the apartment.'

★   ★   ★

By the time the architect arrived, Sam was in a minor state of panic. The whole project seemed too enormous to contemplate. It sounded crazy in cold blood but when she looked out of the window and saw the expanse of intriguing walls and plants, she knew it simply had to be done. She was committed, body and soul.

Jackson's architect, Tony Phelps, was high-powered to say the least. He looked at all the documents and quickly grasped what was needed. At the end of the first day, he had clear ideas on the various stages of planning.

'I recommend you start planning exactly where the entrances, car parks and loos are to be. Allow at least twice as many as you think you'll need. And make certain there's clear access from the road. Get that sorted and the rest will be easy. It's a fascinating project. I'd never have thought you'd go in for anything like this, Jackson.'

'It's the inspiration and enthusiasm of this lady,' Jackson said with a smile at Sam.

'Does that mean she's more than a business acquaintance?' Tony went on.

'Who can tell?' Jackson said enigmatically, and Sam blushed. 'Now, what time would you like to go out for dinner, Samantha? I thought we'd take Tony to that little place we went to recently.'

'Oh, I didn't realise I was invited. I'd like to get Allie settled first. She's still a bit newly back at school.' Suddenly she looked at her watch. 'Look at the time! I'm sorry — you'll have to excuse me — I'm really late for her.'

Jackson told her they would call for her at seven-thirty. Sam felt awkward that Will wasn't invited. He was a vital part of the team and she wished Jackson would set aside his prejudices.

With the help of the diary, Sam had located many landmarks and had the structure and routes of the pathways and drives sorted out. Marguerite often mentioned the visitors who came to stay for the summer and the many carriage rides they had taken.

She discovered that when Henry reached the age of eighteen, he had been eligible to fight in the Great War. Marguerite had tried everything she could think of to enable him to stay on the estate, and her helplessness filled the pages. Finally she had reached her own brave decision. She and Henry would have only one chance and they took it.

As Sam read the words, sharing the girl's despair, it felt as though she were intruding on their privacy. But she couldn't help herself. She felt the tears running down her cheeks. Poor young people. Henry had been killed the following year, probably never knowing that they had conceived a child.

Sam could imagine the horror of the Westcott family when they had realised their daughter was carrying an illegitimate child. The disgrace. Obviously the child had been put out for adoption, possibly surviving to become Will's own grandfather. Perhaps Will could have claimed part of the very estate where he was now the gardener. How times had changed . . . or had they?

Will's Mysterious Past

Next morning, as usual, Allie went outside first thing, hoping to find Jenny. Will was walking by and she called out eagerly, 'Mum's just made some coffee, if you want some.'

'Well now, that sounds very inviting. Do you think she'd mind?'

''Course not. I was wanting to talk to you about Jenny actually.'

They went inside and Allie called out that Will was here. Sam sighed. Her daughter chose the most inopportune moments.

'I'm worried that Jenny's getting very fat, isn't she? I think she needs to go on a diet,' Allie announced.

Will glanced at Sam who shook her head. She hadn't got round to asking Jackson about the puppy.

'I'll think about what you said,' he told Allie. 'A diet may be a good idea.

Now, isn't it time for the school bus? We'll walk you down the drive.'

Jackson watched them from his window. It's quite obvious where *he's* spent the night, he thought sourly, feeling a surge of anger. He hated the idea that Sam might have allowed Will to stay.

'I'd like a word with you, Samantha,' he greeted her formally when she arrived in the office.

'Sure. Any problems?'

'I'm not . . . I mean . . . well, it's rather difficult, but I saw Will coming out of your apartment this morning. I was . . . well, disturbed by the thought of him spending the night with you. With Alison being there, I mean.'

Her eyes flashed. 'How dare you? I'm supposed to ask your permission before having visitors?'

'No, you're right. I apologise. I'm sorry, I was . . . sorry, I'm useless at anything like this. Look, we'd better get to work. I've got the package from Tony Phelps. I'll leave it with you. Check it as soon as you can. I want the planning to go through as fast as possible.'

Sam nodded and opened the package.

'Good grief. It looks like some great town centre development!' she exclaimed.

'It's your project. What I'm paying you for.'

After an hour, her head was aching. She filled the coffee pot and shook out a couple of paracetamol. Why did professionals have to wrap up the simplest things in such incomprehensible jargon? If they could find complicated words to say something, they did.

By lunchtime, she felt even worse and instead of making her usual sandwich, went to lie down for a while. Sleep overtook her until she was woken by the sound of the doorbell. Sleepily she went to open it.

'Are you OK?' Will asked, looking concerned. 'You weren't in the office and I was worried.'

'I'm having my lunch break,' she told

him, wondering what the fuss was about.

'Fine. It's just that you're usually back by one-thirty.'

She glanced at her watch. It was almost three o'clock!

'Good heavens! Allie'll be home in a few minutes.'

'Come and look at the work the builders have done,' Will urged. 'I'm most impressed after so short a time.'

They walked across to the Italian garden, where the transformation was spectacular. The foundations were all complete for the summer-house and pond. Concrete was pouring down a chute from an enormous lorry and being spread in the base of the two structures and along the paths. The builders from the apartments had been sent down to help and within hours the whole scene had changed from chaos into order.

'It's brilliant, Will! It really looks as if we're making progress,' Sam said with uncontrolled enthusiasm.

She went on alone to meet Allie and they walked back to the apartment. Jackson was waiting outside.

'Go in and put the kettle on, will you, love?' Sam told her daughter.

'I'm sorry I flew off the handle this morning,' Jackson said at once. 'I don't want you to think I was prying into your affairs. I didn't mean it to sound like it did. I just . . . hated the thought of you entertaining the gardener for the night. That wasn't why I suggested you move in here.'

Sam was reminded of Marguerite's mother suddenly and almost laughed out loud.

'Aren't you being just a little Victorian-heavy-fatherish about this?'

'He wants to get a ready-made family. You take over where he left his own family. I'd estimate that Alison is just about the right age.'

'What do you mean? He's wonderful with Allie. He loves her. He also claims he loves me. You've hinted before that you know more than you're saying about Will's past. Is it something I should know? If so, you have to tell me.'

'I told you, he worked at the place where . . . where someone I know lives. He was dismissed. He was later proved innocent of the claims made against him but, well, mud sticks, as they say. He came back here and took the gardening job. His wife and child didn't come with him. I don't know what happened to them.'

She continued to stare at him. 'You obviously know more than you're telling me.'

'I'd prefer not to talk about it. Look, why don't you and Alison come and have a meal with me tonight? I know Mrs R. is doing a roast, so there'll be plenty. Save you cooking.'

She shrugged. 'OK, that would be nice. I can work a couple of hours on this and then we'll come through. We won't be able to stay long, of course. Allie has school again tomorrow.'

'Forget about work. Take a break. Relax. Come down in half an hour. I'll tell Mrs R. to expect you.'

'We're going to have supper with Jackson, if that's OK with you,' Sam told Allie when she went indoors.

'Oh good. That means we're sure to have something good. Mrs R.'s the best cook in the world.'

'Well, thanks a bunch!' Sam retorted. 'I do try my best, you know.'

'Yes, but you have to realise that natural cooks are born. You're simply not a natural cook.'

Sam stared. Her daughter was growing up too fast by half.

After a glass of good wine and Mrs Roberts' excellent roast pork, Sam felt totally relaxed. Jackson had been very entertaining and seemed almost light-hearted. He joked with Allie and sent her into peels of laughter. He loved the idea of an opening ceremony once the Italian garden was finished. It was all she could do to stop him phoning immediately to arrange Press coverage.

'Hang on,' Sam laughed. 'We haven't got any building done yet. We can make plans in a few days. But now we must be off. Allie needs to get to bed.'

'How about I bring the brandy bottle along in half an hour or so and we can finish off the meal in style? We could go through the planning stuff together. We need to get it to the next meeting.'

'OK,' Sam agreed. At least it meant she would be able to catch up on some work. 'I'll leave the door on the catch.'

'He's nice, isn't he, Mum?' Allie remarked as she wriggled into her pyjamas. 'In a different sort of way from Will.'

'Very,' Sam agreed.

'Do you like him more than Will?'

'He's different,' she said non-committally. 'Now, young lady, bed.'

★   ★   ★

By the end of the following week, the summer-house was completed. The builders had followed the old photograph perfectly. The foreman was an enthusiast of anything away from his normal routine and had worked carefully to make sure the style was exactly right. The pond would be ready for water in a couple of days, when the proofing had dried out.

'Are we having fish in it?' Allie asked excitedly. 'Where will you get them from and can I come?'

'We'll have to get them from a supplier,' Will replied. 'But we need to get the water settled and a few plants in it before we add the livestock.'

'Livestock? I thought that meant cows and sheep and things.'

'Haven't you heard of water buffalo?' Will asked with a straight face.

'Oh, you,' groaned Allie, realising she was being teased.

'We'll get the plants organised at the start of next week,' Sam decided. 'It'll be good to see something happening. I made a list from what I could recognise in the photograph and one of the old lists I found. Then we'll start work on the bothy. Otherwise the rubble from there will damage the plants we're going to put in.'

Will organised the group of builders they had taken on, who set about the partial demolition of the bothy and were able to work out how the summer-house and the bothy had been linked. Once the stones were cleaned off, it would take a relatively short time to rebuild.

After the new plants were ordered, Sam had some spare time to organise the next stage of the plans. Always, thoughts of the jungle garden seemed to push themselves into her mind but there was too much to be done elsewhere. That particular pleasure would have to wait for a while.

'Busy?' asked Jackson, finding her at her desk for once.

'Nothing pressing. I was just going to look for another site in the garden actually. I think there's some sort of grotto.'

'How on earth do you know that?' he asked suspiciously.

'Something I heard,' she said, a blush

staining her cheeks. Marguerite and Henry were still her secret.

'You're sure you're not a bit psychic?'

Laughing, they went outside into the warm afternoon. She led him across the main lawn, now beginning to recover from the ravages of the diggers.

'Now, round this bit, see? There are heaps of rocks that look as if they've been moved from somewhere else. The ground isn't naturally rocky here.' She disappeared into a pile of undergrowth and saw there was a pathway. She could see masses of ferns growing in the shady darkness and the odd punga stood high over her head.

'Samantha? Are you all right?' called Jackson who had lost sight of her.

'Fine,' came the muffled reply. 'I think we can clear a way through.'

There were crashing sounds as she pushed her way back, and when she emerged, Jackson laughed. 'That shade of green certainly suits you,' he said, pulling her close and wiping the smudge of green moss from her face with his handkerchief. She had bits of twig and foliage in her hair and wore a smile of triumph.

'I knew it! This must be the fern valley. It's supposed to represent a path through the mountains. To give the family and their guests a variety of different places to walk.'

'And your grotto?' Jackson quizzed.

'I'm sure it's there somewhere. I'll go back in with a torch and see what I can find. What's the time?'

'Time for Allie, and the end of everything productive for today, no doubt.'

Sam stared at him. He sounded irritated.

'I'll collect her and we'll come back here and see what we can find once she's changed.'

★ ★ ★

'This is excellent,' Allie announced. 'Intrepid jungle warriors fight their way through insurmountable odds. They

215

hack at the vegetation, undisturbed for centuries . . . '

Armed with a pair of strong secateurs each and a torch, they hacked their way through the overhanging vegetation and came to a wall of solid rock. Groping along for a short way, they felt water trickling down.

'Floods ahead,' called Allie dramatically. 'Waterfalls out of control.'

'Don't go any farther then,' Sam instructed. She was puzzled. As far as she knew, there wasn't any water in this part of the garden. Then she remembered another part of the diary, where Marguerite had written about the irrigation system.

'I think you've made an important discovery,' she told her daughter. 'You've probably saved us all hours of work.'

'It was nothing,' Allie said airily. 'Just consider it my good deed for the day. What have I found?'

'I'm just going to see what's this way,' Sam called over her shoulder, and Allie crashed along behind her.

The smell of damp grew stronger and they came to another heap of rubble. Sam could see some sort of natural formation among the rocks . . . the entrance to what was almost certainly the grotto.

'This is it!' she muttered excitedly. 'The crystal cave! The grotto! I read about it in one of the books or plans or somewhere.'

'It's cold and wet and too dark. Spooky. I don't think I like it much,' complained Allie.

'We'll go back then. I can always come and look at it another time.'

Sam was loath to leave. This was the place she would feel closest to Marguerite and her ill-fated lover.

'Phew,' said Allie when they emerged into the sunshine. 'That was a really weird place. Do you think it was haunted? I could almost feel old-fashioned people in long dresses wandering around.'

Sam stared at her daughter but immediately the mood was dispelled as

Allie grinned at her. 'Come on — race you across the lawn,' she called, setting off at a run.

When Allie was in bed that evening, Sam retrieved her precious diary from the office drawer. She wanted to re-read one of the passages about the grotto. It was another moving piece, one of the last entries in the diary. The words seemed so poignant.

'*I have been feeling unwell for many days now. I cannot explain it. I go each night to our crystal cave. I take a candle and sit in the darkness with just the tiny pool of light providing a small circle where I can feel close to my dear Henry. I hope he thinks of me sometimes. Remembers the night we became man and wife in all but name. The candle shines in our little grotto, the light reflecting from the crystals in the ceiling. It has become our shrine. The shrine to our hopeless love.*

Where are you, Henry? Do you think of me sometimes? My beloved.'

Poor Marguerite. Obviously this had

been written at the start of her pregnancy before she had realised what was happening. There were just a few more entries after that but her final destiny was never mentioned. Sam had looked everywhere she could think of to try to find out what had happened to her. Perhaps she had gone to live with her sister, Rosalie, who had also been widowed during the war. Sam may never know the truth.

Being party to so many secrets from the past gave Sam something of a dilemma. Though she desperately wanted to uncover the grotto for everyone to see, she felt it was almost like exposing a confidence. Suppose she actually found traces of a candle there? It was like opening a shrine to the public gaze. Should she break the trust that had grown between her and Marguerite?

But she was being ridiculous. These people were long gone. Of course the grotto must be opened up.

While the building team worked on

the bothy, she took Will to see her find. There was the irrigation system to look at besides the grotto and the rest of the artificial valley. Will was very excited by the prospect of working out the irrigation system. It added a new dimension to the project. Keeping the many flower-beds and vegetable areas supplied with water had been giving him some headaches. This looked like being the solution, if anyone could ever fathom out how it worked.

'We need to find out exactly where the pipes are. Diggers are notoriously good — or should I say bad — at breaking water pipes.'

'My dad once showed me how to find a water course,' she mentioned.

'How?'

'Divining. I know it sounds like mumbo jumbo, but it works. Well, it did when I was a kid.'

Will grinned at her. 'I'd have thought your father was much too sensible for something like that. He sounds such an interesting man.'

'Maybe it was these odd quirks of irrational thought that made him so interesting.'

'And would he have approved of me?' he asked.

'Oh, I expect so. You're interested in gardening, aren't you?'

'It's not the only thing I'm interested in.' He paused for a moment. 'But maybe you'd like to demonstrate your divining skills. I'm fascinated.'

Sam took up the challenge and went back to the house to find the necessary bits and pieces while Will continued to pull away the vegetation that surrounded the little rocky chasm.

When he saw what she'd brought, he guffawed with laughter. 'You have to be kidding!'

Sam held two empty ballpoint pen cases and two bits of bent wire which she slotted into the plastic. Holding them out in front of her, she began to walk slowly across the ground. They wobbled a bit and suddenly crossed. She picked up a small piece of rock and left it on the ground. She repeated the exercise several times, each time placing a rock at the point where the wires crossed. Soon there was a straight line of rocks stretching along the side of the path.

'That's the start of it, anyhow,' Sam declared.

'I don't believe it! You're *making* the wires move . . . '

'You can blindfold me and lead me if you don't believe it. Here, try it yourself,' Sam offered.

Will took the wires and their holders and began to walk back and forth, just as she'd shown him. Nothing happened.

'Obviously I'm not gifted with the second sight or whatever it is,' he said with a laugh. 'It'll be interesting to see if you're right. When we start digging, we'll make sure you and your bits of bent wire are part of the team.'

'Laugh all you like,' Sam said with a frown. 'You'll see. Now, are we going to try to get closer to this grotto?'

'Grotto?' asked Will, looking puzzled.

'It's just something I found with Allie last night,' she said hurriedly.

'You sure it isn't another case of you and your peculiar insight into this whole place? I'd almost swear that you had inside information.'

'There's nothing strange about it. You'll see one day.'

'I'd better give your theories a try.'

Together they pulled away the larger stones and the little cave-like opening was exposed. The roof was lined with crystals. Sam knew nothing of rocks and couldn't hazard even a guess at what they were, but occasionally, through the dirt of ages, she could see a slight sparkle and feel a roughness beneath her fingers.

'Do you think there may be a spring there?' she asked Will.

'Possibly. More likely the irrigation system has a leak. Curious little place. I wonder what it was for?'

'Just a feature, I expect,' Sam said softly. 'A diversion for the household and their guests. Probably used as a wishing well or something.'

'I expect you're right. Maybe we'll find some old coins.'

There were two paths which converged in front of the grotto. This must be where the two lovers had come to meet in the dusk during that last summer. She shivered, not at the cold but from some deeper emotion. She needed to play a personal role in excavating this particular feature. Men and diggers must not be allowed to get anywhere close.

'I'll get my secateurs and make a start on these bushes,' she said firmly. 'You might like to go and see if you can discover any of the clues to the irrigation system. I'll even lend you my divining rods if you're very good.'

Staring at her thoughtfully, Will nodded. 'I'll leave you to it then.'

An Ambitious Scheme

Once October arrived, Sam and Will began planting spring-flowering bulbs and shrubs. The Italian garden was growing steadily and the pond had been stocked with a variety of fish. Allie counted them every day to make sure none went missing. The pond was still looking particularly vulnerable as most of the water plants were small and not yet providing adequate cover.

Now the bothy was complete, work had begun on clearing out the old greenhouses. There were many more bonfires to get rid of rubbish and tons of broken glass was buried among the hardcore that formed the base for the new concrete. Everywhere looked like a building site and a very long way away from being a garden.

The temptation was always to work in many places rather than concentrate efforts into one area. Curiosity was the main culprit. Everyone wanted to see what lay beneath something and once that happened, there was suddenly a new project to begin.

Jackson made this very point at their next meeting. 'We have to beware of diversifying so much,' he said firmly. 'By all means explore, but I don't want the workmen diverted until the time is right to move on. Now, the Italian garden — I've arranged for the Press and TV to be here on Tuesday next week. I want some decent coverage and plenty of information about future plans.

'Sam, I'd like you to prepare information boards and Will, you're in charge of ensuring proper access to the various sites, ropes round paths and so on. I've organised drinks in a small marquee on the big lawn. That will be delivered on the Monday. That's it. Questions?'

Will and Sam looked blankly at each other and then at Jackson.

'You've rather flung us into this,' Will ventured. 'There's nothing much to see at this time of year.'

'Then it's up to you to make sure there is plenty of information at least. Make the displays colourful to make up for it. Order flowers. Whatever you need. It's not too much to ask, is it? I've ordered canapés and savouries from a company in St Austell and the wine will be delivered at the weekend.'

'You don't leave much to chance,' Sam said.

'You'll be interviewed, of course. Radio. Television. The inspiration behind the project. I suggest you wear something suitably informal, no need to dress up.'

Sam grinned. 'Just as well. I don't have much in my wardrobe — especially not for television. I'm not even sure I can cope. I'm not one for the limelight.'

'You'll be fine. I'll talk you through it nearer the time. That's it for now. I have to be away for the next four days.' Jackson shut his notebook with a snap and half rose from his seat. 'Everything is all right, isn't it?'

'I'm sure it will be. I s'pose you've organised the guest list too?' Sam asked with the slightest hint of annoyance.

'The list's in your folder. Add anyone else you think should be included. Friends, important local folk — you know the sort of thing. I have to dash now. Call the London office if you need to contact me.' He whirled out, leaving Sam and Will almost open-mouthed in shock.

'So that's how it's done in the big wide world,' Will said slowly. 'I hope no-one's going to be disappointed. There isn't much to see yet.'

'You heard the man — make posters and displays big and colourful. How the dickens am I going to make posters and display boards? My art is pretty pathetic at the best of times. Even Allie can draw things better than me.'

'Maybe that's it. Get Allie and some of her friends to draw pictures of magic gardens or something.'

'Giant exotic flowers — yes. We can cut them out and stick them on boards or card — maybe use them as way pointers or something. And we could make a jungle collage to represent our plans for the valley. Maybe the school would do some during their art lesson. I'll phone the Head and ask.'

'You have exactly one week and a day,' Will pointed out.

'Then we'll have to abandon all actual gardening for the next week. This is our first public awareness day and we have to make it work.'

★　★　★

The next few days were a frenzy of activity. The Head made an announcement about the flower-making and the children could work at play-times if they wished.

It was a great success and soon Allie's friends were sending in lots of huge flowers on long bendy stalks, and Sam promised that everyone who had joined in would be invited to see the garden once the official part of the day was over.

The library was covered in large pieces of heavy card and any pictures, bits of information or anything else useful was dumped there. Mrs Roberts gave up all attempts to clean or work anywhere other than the kitchen.

As Sam was seeing Allie to bed one evening, the phone rang. It was her brother. 'Hi, sis. How's it going?'

'Phil! It's lovely to hear from you. Everything's frantic here. Jackson's sprung this 'do' on us.' She continued to tell him the plan and filled him in on all the work they were doing. 'Anyway, I don't suppose you really wanted to know all that,' she said. 'Is there a special reason you called?'

'I'm going to Exeter on business on Friday. I thought I might drive on down to see you for the weekend. What do you think?'

'Oh, Phil . . . I'd love to see you, but it's such a busy time. I wouldn't have much time to spend with you. Can't you make it some other time?'

'I won't come if you don't want me to. I just thought it would be nice to see what sort of trouble my big sister's got herself into.'

'Of course I want to see you. Look, just come — I expect it'll be fine. I'm just panicking a bit at the moment. I'm suddenly in charge of something I haven't the foggiest idea how to cope with. Have you ever organised an exhibition?'

'All the time,' Phil said reassuringly. 'Seriously, love, I can help. I'll be with you in time for dinner on Friday. Maybe I can take my favourite sister and niece out for a meal?'

'Are my cousins and Auntie Jane coming as well?' Allie wanted to know.

'I forgot to ask,' Sam replied stupidly. 'What am I like?'

'Good job you've got me to organise you, isn't it?' the child said with a shake of her head. 'You really are hopeless, Mum. I suppose you have remembered my birthday's in a few weeks?'

'Of course I have, darling,' Sam said, crossing her fingers as she told the small fib. When would she ever have time to organise something for that? 'You'll have to let me know what you want. I was going to get a CD player but now you have one, I'll have to think again.'

'There is one thing I *really* want,' she said.

'What's that?' Sam asked, knowing the answer already

'A dog,' Allie said predictably.

'I'll think about it,' Sam promised, cursing herself that she had still forgotten to ask Jackson's permission. 'I suspect you have a reason for asking? Anything to do with Jenny?'

'Well . . . I did think she was getting a bit fat and most females get fat when they're pregnant, so I asked Will and he said yes. We don't know who she mated with so we don't know what the pups will be like. But it won't matter, will it?

Maybe we could have one of Jenny's puppies? Please, Mum.'

'If Jackson agrees, of course we can. But you'll have to be the one who looks after it. Feed it and exercise it, and clear up any messes.'

'Right! My puppy won't make messes though,' Allie said with misplaced confidence.

Sam worked hard all week, continuing late into the evenings. Allie helped with the various posters and they got thoroughly messy with paint and glue. She hoped the results would look sufficiently professional for Jackson's high standards. She wanted to provide simple statements about their intentions for the garden and let the site tell its own story.

She had been delighted with a package of photographs from Jackson. There were enlargements of the many shots he had taken during the work. It was all coming together well and by late Thursday evening, she felt satisfied.

Will looked in before breakfast on Friday morning to announce that Jenny had produced a litter of five pups during the night. They all had her markings and colourings in some form or other. Whoever the father had been, the pups were obviously dominated by their mother's genes.

'Can I come and see them?' Allie demanded.

'Come after school. Jenny needs to rest for a while now. She's very tired and might get cross if she's disturbed.'

'But I wanted to see them while they're still very new! I want to choose which one to have for my very own,' Allie protested.

'We don't even know if Jackson will let us have one. Puppies are very messy creatures, you realise.' Sam needed to prepare the girl, just in case Jackson disappointed them.

'Please — can't I just take a peek?' she begged.

'Just a quick look then,' Will allowed. 'But you mustn't even try to touch

234

them or Jenny might decide she'll reject them.'

'Why would she do that?' Allie asked curiously. 'I thought all mothers loved their children.'

'Of course most mothers love their babies, but sometimes, with animals, something can put them off.'

'That's weird. I thought it was only fathers who didn't want their babies.'

Sam and Will exchanged a glance. Plainly Allie had buried some of her thoughts about her own father deep inside herself.

'Dogs are different,' Sam began. 'They don't settle down with another dog. Not like people.' She realised she was on the road to nowhere and probably making things worse.

Will saw her difficulty and stepped in quickly. 'You'd better hurry and eat that toast if you want even the quickest peek now. I'll go and wait at my house for you. Don't be long or you'll miss the bus.'

Sam shot him a look of gratitude.

Everything she had been trying to say had gone rather wrong, especially in relation to her own marriage with Allie's father.

'I've never seen you move so quickly,' commented Sam when Allie appeared all ready for school five minutes later. 'Pity Jenny doesn't have puppies every day.'

They went across the damp lawn to Will's lodge and opened the door softly. He was in the porch with the dogs and motioned them to be quiet. In a small, closed-off corner, Jenny was lying in her bed with the snuffling heap of tiny pups in a bundle beside her, small patches of black-covered pink skin that had hardly any fur. Tiny paws and noses were all mixed up together, so it was almost impossible to see how many there were.

'They don't look much like dogs, do they?' Allie whispered.

'Just wait a few days and you'll soon see,' Will whispered back. He pointed towards the door and Sam nodded, pulling Allie's hand gently.

'School time,' Sam said. 'Uncle Phil will be here this evening, don't forget. He's taking us out for a meal.'

★   ★   ★

Sam checked everything possible was ready for their grand opening. She hadn't heard from Jackson since he had left after their meeting. She dreaded the thought of the television interview.

She spent the afternoon outside. Presently, deep in thought and covered in earth, she became aware of a commotion nearby. There was a lorry driving over the lawn. In horror, she rushed over. The ground was just recovering from the last onslaught and it needed to look good for Tuesday.

What on earth was it? She went closer to take a look. Some sort of *house* was being delivered.

'You the boss?' called the driver from his cab.

'Well, sort of. I s'pose so. What on

earth have you got there?'

'Office, love. Well, half of it, I should say.'

'Half an office?' Sam spluttered. 'Why?'

'Don't ask me. I'm only the driver. Ordered in the name of Clark. To be delivered here at Pengelly Hall.'

She stood nonplussed for a moment. Where on earth should it go? And why hadn't the wretched man warned her? He could at least have telephoned to let her know it was arriving.

Just as she was about to direct the driver to the other side of the house, a second lorry drove in through the gates.

'Here's your other half, love. Now we're in business. Put them together and you can move in right away. Right — where did you want them?'

Before she could reply, she heard the distinctive beat of a helicopter approaching. It could only be one person. Trust Jackson to do things in style!

'Hang on a minute. I think the real boss has arrived,' she said, pointing upwards. 'He'll tell you exactly where he wants it. It might be a good idea if you moved your lorry off the grass though. It's supposed to be a lawn.'

Wearing a dark business suit, looking quite inappropriate for the surroundings, Jackson hurried across the grass.

'Good, they've arrived. I'd hoped to get here first but you know how things are. What do you think?'

She laughed. 'What am I supposed to think? Shock? Horror?'

He looked offended. 'Excuse me but I did a very good deal and couldn't turn it down. I thought they would fit in the corner over there, under the trees. OK with you?'

She shrugged. 'Why bother to ask? You obviously know what you want. It would have been nice to be warned though,' she added pointedly.

'Sorry, no time. OK,' he said turning to the drivers, 'over there, please. What help do you need to unload this lot?'

Within a few minutes, one of the diggers had been brought over and the low-loader had backed into place. Feeling like a child watching workers on a building site, Sam stood gawping. It took only a short time before the two halves of the building were being bolted together and a sizeable office block was in place. Jackson had obviously seen the flat piece of ground and some instinct had told him it would be large enough for the structure.

'What do you think?' he said enthusiastically. 'We'll build proper offices when the main site is up and running. Tax deductible, of course, once we're flourishing.'

'I get the feeling that our motivations are quite different,' Sam said doubtfully. 'I'm looking at the restoration more as a working museum. You see it as just another business venture.'

'That's why we make a good team,' he assured her. 'You provide the artistic side and I provide the business sense.'

It was only an hour and a half since she had been quietly weeding, she reflected. Now she was standing looking at a new office block. Jackson Clark was capable of taking anyone's breath away.

As she rounded the corner of the house, a large car stopped beside her. To her surprise, Allie was in the passenger seat and Phil climbed out of the driving seat.

'Hi, sis. I made it earlier than I thought. I found this stray at the gate and took pity on her. She seems to be carrying half a forest with her. She assured me you're expecting it!'

'Phil, it's wonderful to see you.' They hugged each other and chatted excitedly. Phil was most impressed with the Hall and couldn't wait to see round the whole place.

'We should do outside first,' Allie instructed, 'or it'll be too dark to see anything. Come on, I'll show you the way.' She grabbed her uncle's hand and dragged him off, telling him the details of the various projects.

When she spotted the office block, she stopped dead in her tracks. 'What on earth is that?' she squealed.

'Offices,' Sam returned. 'It arrived a couple of hours ago.'

They opened one of the side doors and found themselves in a carpeted foyer. There was a small reception area and various doors leading off it. There were four sizeable rooms, each with electric and phone sockets, heaters, and a window.

'Phew,' said Phil. 'Talk about instant building. This is really good.'

'How do the sockets work?' asked Allie. 'Don't you need to have proper electricity?'

Phil explained how it would work while Sam wandered round, trying to decide which of the rooms she would prefer to use.

'Your Jackson Clark sounds like quite a guy,' Phil commented. 'I've heard of him, of course, and we use some of his products. He's a very sound business-man — it's no fly-by-night company that'll go bust in five minutes.'

'Thanks for the vote of confidence,' Jackson said as he came into the room.

He held out a hand and introduced himself. 'So, you've used our software, have you? What's your line?'

While he and Phil began to talk the sort of business that left Sam feeling quite ignorant, she and Allie wandered off.

It was becoming darker and Allie was getting impatient. They rejoined the men and Phil put his arm affectionately round his sister.

'I think you've done brilliantly, Sam,' he said. 'What an amazing project. I always did think you should do something in horticulture. You shared Dad's interest and his knack for making things grow. It all sounds very exciting, Jackson. Very perceptive of you.'

'It's all due to Sam's enthusiasm, I assure you. I've had this place for three years and I'd never even walked round half of it till she came on the scene.'

'I think we should be getting inside,' Sam suggested. 'Phil hasn't even seen the apartment or anything.'

'Let's all have dinner,' suggested

Jackson. 'I need to catch up on the details for Tuesday.'

'Uncle Phil's taking me and Mum out somewhere, aren't you?'

'I'd be pleased to do the honours,' Jackson replied.

'Thanks all the same, but I think I'd like this evening to catch up on the family,' Sam said. 'We can discuss work some other time. Tomorrow morning, maybe? Just for an hour or so. I think we're quite up to speed.'

Jackson looked slightly annoyed but gave a shrug. 'As you like. I'd hate to intrude on family. Maybe I'll see you in the morning. I'm not sure of my plans yet.' He turned away to his own apartment.

'Am I missing something?' Phil asked. 'He sounded quite put out.'

'Ignore it. He just likes to organise everyone and gets cross if people try to have a life of their own,' Sam explained.

'They're both after her,' Allie announced.

'Don't be ridiculous,' Sam spluttered.

'Both?' Phil queried. 'Are you saying my sister's become a man-eater?'

'Come off it!' Sam protested. 'I'd be lucky to get a second glance from a cross-eyed puppy!'

'Jackson does like you quite a lot,' Allie put in. 'He looks at you all gaga. A bit like Will does sometimes.'

'Will?' asked Phil, his eyebrows raised in curiosity.

Sam frowned slightly. 'Someone I work with.'

'Can I go and see Jenny and my puppy?' Allie asked suddenly. 'Where will it sleep? We haven't got a bed for it or anything.'

Sam smiled and explained that pups couldn't leave their mothers for several weeks. Allie's face fell. In her eyes, the puppy was already hers and quite ready to play and run around.

* * *

The next morning was very busy. Phil went to meet Lucinda Johns, who

245

inevitably poured forth a flood of memories about them as children.

They spent the rest of the morning exploring the garden. Phil gasped at the magnitude of the undertaking. He also had the business sense to realise that Jackson's own involvement was essential.

'I wish he would talk through his plans before he gets everything finalised, though,' Sam complained. 'This opening on Tuesday, for instance. He's organised television people to come. He wants to get people interested so that any planning applications will go through more easily.'

'Sound thinking,' Phil commented.

'Yes, but he expects me to do an interview. But I'll be useless! Tongue-tied and looking like a great fat hen.'

'Rubbish! You're looking wonderful, Sam. Better than I can ever remember. Life here suits you.'

'You'll be fine,' Allie chipped in. 'I wouldn't mind. In fact, it'll be wicked.

Everyone at school will be dead jealous.'

'Over to you then, with the greatest of pleasure.'

'I think that would be a great idea,' came a voice from behind them and Jackson appeared on the terrace carrying a tray and an ice bucket and some glasses. 'I thought we ought to test the champagne,' he added. He set down the tray on a low wall and expertly popped the cork and filled some glasses. 'There you are, Samantha. And Phil. Do you want some, Alison?'

'No fear! It's horrible stuff. And please don't call me Alison. It sounds as if you're really cross with me. Everyone calls me Allie. Is it OK if I go and see Jenny and the puppies now?' she asked, turning to her mother. Sam nodded and the child skipped off happily.

'I'd like to chat to you, Phil, if you have the time. Run a few ideas past you,' Jackson said.

'Sure,' Phil replied, 'though I doubt that I'm quite in your league.'

'Any chance of you staying on for a few days? You should be here on Tuesday.' He turned to Sam. 'I think the idea of *Allie*,' he stressed the word, 'appearing with you on the TV interview is excellent. It'll give you confidence and, as she keeps telling me, if it wasn't for her, you may never have found the garden in the first place.'

'I'm not sure about that but, yes, it would be nice. I'll see if she can be let off school for a couple of hours. So, Phil? What about staying on?'

'Do you know, I just might.'

Phil and Jackson went into the office, into what Allie described as a huddle over the computers. They talked for some time and when he finally came out again, Phil was looking most impressed.

'It's absolutely inspiring,' he said cheerfully. 'I think it's a unique project. And it'll probably make a fortune besides being something very worthwhile. Now, are we going to have a proper look round?'

They spent the rest of the day

wandering in the valley, Sam pointing out the trees they had found during their first walks through Allie's magic forest.

'Do you remember any of this from when we were kids?' Sam asked.

'No, but when did we have time for anything but the beach? But I do remember Dad wandering off. In fact, I think I remember him talking about some garden. Maybe he did find it and never told us. It would be nice to think he did,' he mused. 'It would give it an added dimension if his daughter were to be the one to restore it all.' He smiled at her. 'It's good to see you happy again. Now, who's this Will Allie talks about so often? Do I get to meet him? Give him my seal of approval?'

'I'm not sure where he is. He'll be around after the weekend, of course.'

'And do I detect a hint of romance in the air?'

'Shut up,' Sam hissed. 'Allie's always pushing us together. Don't give her any more ideas. I'm happy as I am.'

'With two adoring males in attendance? I should think so!'

'You're being ridiculous. Will is — I know he would like it to be something more. Jackson — well, no-one can get really close to him. He's an enigma. He and Will seem to hate each other for some reason. Each warns me about the other.'

They continued their chat, lowering their voices whenever Allie was in range, though she spent most of her time dancing in and out of the trees, lost in some imaginary world of her own. When Sam asked her what game she was playing, she explained that she was practising games to play with the puppy when she came.

The next two days seems to flash by. Will got on well with Phil, though he seemed rather quiet and a little preoccupied for much of the time.

For most of Monday they all worked to prepare the exhibition. Jackson appreciated the children's flowers, not for the quality of the work but for the fresh innocence of it all. It was excellent publicity. A whole different group of people would become interested. He insisted that the whole school should be invited to visit the project as soon as possible.

'It'll be a good follow-up for the TV people. Are you all set for the interview in the morning?'

'I still haven't decided what I should wear. I only like wearing jeans.'

'So, wear jeans. Be comfortable. Who cares about anything else? I think they're quite appropriate in the circumstances.'

'Great. I thought you'd hate the idea. I thought you'd want me to look all smart and business-like.'

He shook his head. 'You're a unique and genuine human being, not some sort of office clone.' He turned to the new office block, but then turned back again almost immediately. 'Did anyone think of ordering some Portaloos?' he demanded. 'We'd better get on to it straight away.'

Sam blinked. What a man!

Secrets Revealed

The following morning was glorious, everything they could have hoped for. The trees had turned into shimmering banks of autumn colour, illuminated by the low sun. The school-children's bright flowers had been stuck on to canes and lined the route from the temporary car park to the Italian garden.

The marquee had been decorated with pictures and posters and tables of drinks stood ready. A couple of the girls from the village had been brought in to act as waitresses, trained rigorously by Mrs Roberts.

Two complicated flower arrangements stood on pedestals at each side of the entrance to the garden itself and planters of bright geraniums had been placed around the pond.

Sam fiddled with everything she

stood next to, a bundle of nerves about the coming ordeal. Allie was joyfully getting in everyone's way, thrilled to be a part of it all and to be missing school into the bargain.

The TV van arrived and Sam rushed to the loo for at least the ninth time since breakfast.

However, when the producer introduced himself to her, she felt immediately at ease once he had explained that the film could be edited and there would be no problem if she froze, said the wrong thing or did something she didn't like. She felt much better at once.

They filmed various bits of the garden, led by Allie who had assumed the role of guide-in-chief and came to do the interview with Sam in the restored Italian garden. They would mix bits of film and shots of her and Jackson. Will was also going to play his part and they even managed to take some footage of the puppies.

'After all, Jenny was quite an important part of it all, wasn't she,

Mum?' Allie told the cameraman.

Once the TV people had finished the Press came forward, taking several photographs of Allie and her mother in various parts of the garden. Then Jackson did his piece, stressing the need for a quick decision on the planning application.

Once the interviews were over, the invited guests began to arrive. Sam felt as if her smile was frozen on to her face. The whole thing had caught everyone's imagination and several people claimed to know someone who knew someone who'd worked there at one time, though they were a little less clear when Sam asked them for specific names and addresses.

It was well into the afternoon before everyone had gone. By then Sam felt totally drained. Allie was busily emptying all the bottles into a large jug and gathering up the empty plates.

'What are you doing with all that wine?' Jackson asked.

'I thought we could use it to make

cocktails for this evening,' she said cheerfully. 'Save opening any more later.' He stared after her with a smile and a shake of his head.

Sam felt that Will had been avoiding them for the past few days. She assumed it was something to do with the puppies or his involvement with the extra work for the opening. There seemed to be some barrier between them. Or perhaps it was because of Phil and the time she was spending with him. In any case, in an attempt to bridge the gap, she had invited Will to share Phil's last evening. He had been persuaded, though without enthusiasm.

When Jackson also invited them out to dinner, he was annoyed that Sam expected Will to join them.

'I've already invited him to come to us,' Sam said.

'But I want to talk to you and Phil. Can't you un-invite him?'

'He's been feeling left out as it is,' she began. 'Anyway, that would be plain rude.'

'I suppose you'd better invite him as well then. He's a good worker but there's a lot lacking in his social skills.'

'How dare you?' Sam protested, but he looked unconcerned.

'I told you — invite him. It doesn't really matter, does it?'

However, when Sam passed on the invitation, Will's reaction was even more negative and he accused her of trying to organise him.

'I'd rather see you another evening,' he declared. 'When life has settled down again. Do you need a sitter for Allie?'

'It's OK, Mrs Roberts will listen for her.'

As Will strode off, Sam gave a sigh. 'Ah, well, I did my best,' she muttered.

'I want to talk to you on a business matter,' Jackson said rather formally to Phil over the dinner table that evening. 'I'd like you to consider an idea. Once this project is up and running, the whole venture will become a major concern. Bigger than anything we'd planned. Talking to the Press and TV chaps the other day has convinced me. I'd like you to join the team as our financial director, Phil. Business manager, perhaps. You have the sort of drive that we could use. And I can always find a place for a good accountant in my other business if it does fall flat — which it won't, of course. I'm sure Samantha would be delighted to have some of her family nearer to her. Discuss it with your wife.'

Phil's face was a picture. He looked at Sam. 'Did you have anything to do with this?'

She held up her hands in a gesture of innocence. 'Not me. It's as much a surprise to me as it is to you. I'm not sure what Jane will think, but I anticipate that this is going to be quite some project by the time we're finished.'

'Live here in Cornwall? It's very tempting. How soon do you need an answer?' Phil had begun to grin. 'I've missed you, sis. It would be great to be near again.'

'Think about it,' Jackson urged. 'I'll jot down a few figures for you to consider and you can let me know by the end of the week. Now, more wine, anyone?'

Sam and Phil both got a little drunk, excitedly chatting about the possibilities before them, and by the time Jackson drove them home they were convinced in their own minds that the future was all but settled.

As Phil drove away the next morning, Sam felt no real sense of loss, convinced that he would soon be moving to Cornwall. Allie would be thrilled to have her cousins living nearby. She had missed them.

★　★　★

'My sister-in-law certainly sounds enthusiastic,' Sam reported to Jackson after several calls.

'I should think so. I offered him a very attractive package. And if he doesn't want one of the apartments, he can look around for something else. It's the council planning meeting today, isn't it? We should get the answer we're waiting for.'

'Or they'll turn us down flat and we'll have wasted everyone's time,' she said gloomily.

'Nonsense. I never lose anything I really want,' he said with a laugh, and she stared at him, knowing he wasn't entirely joking. 'Come on, let's decide how we'll celebrate.'

They spent the rest of the day working on various ideas but all the time were waiting for the phone to ring. Jackson had persuaded one of the council's administration staff to let him know as soon as there was any news.

'We have to make some arrangement with a good nursery,' Sam told him. 'We need so much it'll cost an absolute fortune to stock even the few beds that are ready. Eventually I want to grow most of our own stuff.' She had made a list of plants for some herbaceous borders and was still reeling from the projected cost.

'I've been giving this some thought,' Jackson replied, tilting his chair back. 'I thought I'd call in a few favours. What we need is sponsorship. I think it could become a major tourist attraction and loads of people will want to be associated with it. I'm also putting in for some European grants, Lottery money, environmental research . . . you name it.'

Sam stared. He was obviously looking much farther ahead than she was. All she was hoping was that the council would approve their outline plans and give permission to change the use of the site. Apart from new exit and entrance sites, the plans included modest car-parking space and some public toilets. But for Jackson, this was only the start of something way beyond her own imagination.

The phone rang. Jackson snatched it up.

'Yes?' He listened for a moment.

'You've got to be kidding! Darned bureaucrats. Petty-minded little bigots. Right — well, thanks anyhow.' He slammed the phone down and glared at Sam.

'Seems the council have decided in their wisdom that we do not have a sufficiently well-placed site for access to the main routes. Though in principle they like the idea, they feel obliged to turn down the plan in its present form. We must submit revised plans showing a more sympathetic consideration of the local environment.'

'So that's it?' Sam said, disappointment clearly in her voice.

'Not likely! We're going to appeal. We can say our projections for visitor numbers may have been exaggerated and . . . oh, there are all sorts of things we can do. I'll get straight on to Tony Phelps now. He'll sort it out. Meantime, I suggest you contact local growers and see what sort of deal you can get for our basic starter plants. You'd better get a few polytunnels ordered. If you plan to grow our own stuff, the sooner it's started, the better.' He was dialling the architect as he spoke and Sam was left almost breathless at his working pace. A refusal of planning permission? What did that matter to the mighty Jackson Clark?

'You heard anything from the council yet?' Will asked when she ran into him a few minutes later.

'Bad news, I'm afraid. Something about poor access routes.'

'That's that then. I can't see Jackson being allowed to build a three-lane motorway to reach this place. What's going to happen now?'

'According to him, we simply re-apply with a few changes. He's talking it through with Tony Phelps right now. Meanwhile I'm instructed to order plants and several polytunnels. Nothing's changed. Oh, and we're going for grants from every source on the planet. You have to admit, this man isn't used to doing things by halves.'

There was a definite hint of admiration

in her voice, Will noticed, and his expression changed. This whole business was beginning to get out of hand. Gardening shouldn't be stressful and demanding like this.

'Sam, please be careful. You seem to be getting very involved.'

'What do you expect?'

'I don't just mean in the project. That man's no good for you.'

'You're getting your wires crossed, Will. He's not remotely interested in me, nor me in him. Now, I'd better get back.' She turned away from him.

'Sam, wait.' Flinging his garden fork down he stepped towards her and grabbed her hands. Pulling her to him he held her tightly and bent his head to kiss her.

'Will, no — don't. Stop it!' She pushed him away angrily. 'What do you think you're doing?' she demanded.

'Sam, I love you. You know I do. Aren't I good enough for you?' His clear blue eyes were clouded with emotion. He looked desperate. 'It's him, isn't it? You want the man with the money.'

'Oh, Will, don't spoil everything. I like you a lot and Allie adores you. Please, don't lay all this on me. I have enough to think about at the moment — I haven't got room for a personal life as well.'

'You think you may have a chance with Jackson though, don't you? Well, I sincerely hope you don't get hurt by our boss but don't allow yourself to expect anything.'

Sam stared. 'I . . . I'm sorry. I must get back. Loads to do,' she mumbled as she rushed away, blinking hard to force back the threatening tears.

'Hi, Mum. You going somewhere?' Allie asked when Sam met her on the drive.

'No, darling, I just saw it was time for you to come home and thought I'd meet you.'

'What's wrong?' Allie asked suspiciously. 'Have you been crying?'

'Nothing. I do love you, Allie.' Sam

bent to hug her and held her close for a moment. 'Don't you ever forget that, will you?'

''Course not,' Allie said quickly. 'Though you must admit, you're not usually this soppy. Has Mrs Roberts been baking today? I'll just go and see if she's all right.'

Sam watched as she ran into the house. She also noticed that Allie spared time to wave to Will, who was still standing watching.

* * *

The amended plans were registered within days of the first meeting and they had high hopes of success this time. They wasted no time in clearing more ground and more areas were planted. Jackson spent much of his time at his computer or on the telephone, though he developed the habit of walking down to the main working sites towards the end of each day, to see the progress, as he put it.

'I want to begin a routine of meetings at least once a week,' he announced on the day of the vital council meeting. 'We each need to know what the others are doing and set targets for the coming week. I suggest Monday mornings at ten. That will give you time to get the work started before the meeting and maximise on the labour we'll have coming in.'

'Sounds good,' Sam responded. 'I was thinking we need to co-ordinate things a bit more as time moves on.'

'Tell Will, please. In fact, we'll have a briefing today. Ask Mrs Roberts to organise lunch, will you? For the three of us. And we'll need the whole afternoon to cover everything. Clear your desk, please, and get Will to make himself available. We have a secretary starting on Monday, by the way, so that'll save us time.'

'A secretary? Whatever for?'

'Typing. Reception duties. Phone. All the usual stuff.'

'But I can do most of that, surely?'

'You won't have time and it's wasting your talents.'

'The man's a megalomaniac,' snapped Will when she told him. 'Power crazy. What's he aiming for? A rival for Kew Gardens?'

'Don't snap at me — I'm only the messenger.'

'OK, I'll be at the house at one: scrubbed fingernails, clean shirt and tie. See you then.'

★　★　★

The lunch table was set formally in the old library. Will came in, obviously having taken a shower. Damp tendrils of hair curled at his neck and he had a fresh shirt on, though without the promised tie. Jackson came in, three professional-looking folders in his hand. He gave them one each and without even asking poured glasses of white wine for each of them.

'Right,' he said in a business-like way. 'We have a lot to discuss. I'm hopeful

267

that the council meeting will go our way this time so I wanted to bring you both up to speed with the project.'

Sam and Will exchanged glances as Mrs Roberts came into the room carrying a large tureen.

'The soup's ready, if you don't mind sitting down now.' Her voice was slightly brusque and Sam could sense an unusual, suppressed anger in her.

'Thank you, Mrs Roberts,' Sam said rather pointedly. 'You're amazing to provide all this at such short notice.' She was rewarded with a beaming smile and was it just the ghost of a wink?

They sat and Jackson began his presentation even before the first mouthful of the delicious asparagus soup had been swallowed.

By the end of the meal, both Will and Sam's minds were reeling. Every possible source of grants had been accessed and there were packages of application forms, filled in and with copies for each of them in the folders. Jackson and his London office staff had been very busy.

The major shock was the main workforce he was proposing to use. He had contacted a number of agencies and residential homes in the area, all of which worked with disabled people and those with learning difficulties.

'I see it this way,' he began. 'Lots of folk with learning difficulties are perfectly competent to do simple manual tasks. This project would give them motivation and worthwhile work to do. It's fully in line with government policies. Will, I think you're the perfect person to take charge of this side of the business. I'll sort out a new contract, of course, and there will obviously be a suitable salary package to go with it,' he concluded.

'I'll have to give it some thought,' Will responded cautiously. 'I'd left this sort of thing behind me. But, in principle, it sounds a good idea.'

Sam. slowly drained her coffee cup and eyed Jackson.

'Why use people with learning

269

difficulties? I find it hard to believe it's purely altruistic. What's in it for you, apart from a cheap source of labour?'

His eyes flashed slightly. 'I'd like to provide this opportunity. There's little enough employment for anyone locally, let alone anyone with disabilities. I'm not all bad, you know, Samantha.'

'I'm sure you're not,' she muttered. 'But I'd hate to think of claims of exploitation being levelled at us.'

The discussion continued well into the afternoon. Eventually Mrs Roberts arrived to say there was an important phone call for Mr Clark.

'The council,' Sam breathed. 'With all of this, I'd forgotten we're waiting to hear from them.'

When Jackson returned, his expression told them they'd been successful. He was followed by Mrs Roberts, bearing a tray with four champagne glasses and a bottle of Bollinger in an ice bucket.

'We've done it!' Jackson said unnecessarily. 'Permission granted exactly as we hoped.'

He popped the cork and they toasted the project, Mrs Roberts also being given a glass of champagne, though she managed to look rather ill-at-ease as she sipped.

'Here's to all of us,' Jackson said. 'An unbeatable team. You too, Mrs R. You're the power behind us all. Well done, everyone!'

'Nothing can stop us now,' Sam said happily.

'Well done, Sam,' Will enthused. He gave her a hug and for once she didn't draw away. She even seemed to respond. He felt stupidly encouraged by the small gesture until the same response was given to Jackson.

'I didn't quite finish all my suggestions,' Jackson said after a few minutes. 'Sam, I want you to take on an increased role as estate manager. Overall charge of the entire project. When Phil comes down to join us next month, he'll see to the financial side and you'll work closely with him. Don't worry about being away from the dirty-hands side of things. You'll have the pleasure of discovery without the hard labour. What do you say?'

'I appreciate your confidence, Jackson, but it's all way beyond my experience. Besides, there's Allie to think of. Oh lord, Allie!' Sam wailed. 'She'll be home from school!' How could she have got so involved that she'd forgotten the most important thing in her life. 'Allie? Where are you?' she called, darting from the room.

'Why are you yelling, Mum?' Allie asked, appearing in the corridor.

'Oh, Allie. Where were you?' Sam asked.

'In the kitchen getting a biscuit. I always go there first when I get home.'

'But Mrs R. was with us, celebrating getting the planning passed.'

'Yes, but I know where the biscuits are kept. And a glass of milk. Mrs R. lets me get it myself.' The milky moustache above her mouth was still visible. 'Don't fuss, Mum! Can I go and see my puppy now? Will says she'll be able to come home next week. I've called her Millie, by the way.'

'That's a lovely name. But first let's go and see if Jackson and Will have finished all the champagne.'

★   ★   ★

Sam went into the office and looked at the plan of the site she had pinned up on the wall. She had never dreamed that first afternoon when she and Allie had discovered their 'magic forest' that all this could happen.

'Penny for them?' Jackson asked as he came into the office.

'I'm sure you can guess,' she replied.

'I wanted to talk to you in private,' he swept on. 'About my plans for the workforce. Do you still think I'm trying to be exploitative?'

'Frankly, yes,' Sam said bluntly. 'Why not simply employ local people?'

'It's a personal thing. Maybe I should explain to you what's behind it.'

'I want to hear, Jackson, but not now.

It'll soon be Allie's suppertime. Come and have coffee after she's gone to bed.'

Needing some fresh air, she went for a walk. The nights were drawing in and she gave a slight shiver. Her thoughts drifted towards Marguerite and her lover. They had met here, in what they had called the jungle garden. She closed her eyes. She was becoming a romantic idiot, imagining ghosts, allowing her imagination to run riot. How Jackson would despise her if he knew.

She knew she could never share the secret diary with him. Sharing it would somehow sully Marguerite's memory. But the garden would bear a much stronger resemblance to the original if she allowed herself to follow the diary.

'Goodnight, Marguerite and Henry,' she whispered as she crept away.

Her contemplative mood was broken as she met her daughter.

'Jenny and Millie are such good friends, Mum,' Allie said cheerfully. 'I'm so relieved. I couldn't bear to hurt Jenny's feelings by having another dog around. What's for tea?'

Sam struggled to bring herself back to the reality of life. Marguerite would never have heard of fish fingers, burgers or baked beans.

★ ★ ★

'I could do with a brandy,' Jackson announced as he sat down in her living-room later.

Sam poured a large measure into a glass and handed it to him. 'Do you want some coffee to go with that?' she asked, but he shook his head.

'You wanted to tell me something,' Sam prompted as she settled down in her favourite armchair.

He nodded, then, after a pause, began. 'When I — we — began this project, I saw it as an interesting diversion. My life has been all about machines, computers. Then you came along like a breath of fresh air. You believed in your project; you seemed focussed. I was once like that. The products I designed were popular, just at the time the market was expanding. I'd never have believed how successful it all could be.'

'What does this have to do with your plans?'

'It's a personal thing. This is difficult. I never talk to anyone . . . but it seems necessary that you understand everything.'

'I'm flattered that you feel able to talk to me,' she said softly.

'You're easy to confide in.' He paused. 'One reason I drove myself was for my brother.'

'I didn't know you had a brother,' Sam commented.

'He's a . . . a difficult man. He's autistic. I don't know if you're aware of what that means?'

'Not really. It's something to do with being unable to communicate, isn't it?'

'In some ways, but it's more complicated than that. He lives in his own world much of the time. He's obsessed with a few specific things and talks about them non-stop. He can be quite exhausting. There's virtually no affection between us. We never played together as children.'

Sam thought of her own brother and the deep love between them.

'How did that affect your parents?' she wondered.

'They didn't know how to cope,' he admitted. 'They eventually pushed me off to boarding-school when I was seven. I was being difficult, they said.'

'And how did that affect you?'

'I suppose I became determined to survive and to organise my life, to have full control of my own future. My parents died when I was in my final year at university. I had to become responsible for all sorts of things, including Dominic.'

'How did you cope with that?'

'I made sure I would have enough money to provide residential care for him. I used most of my parents' estate to secure him a suitable place, and the bit left over I put into my first business enterprise. I'd always been good with electronics and was into computers early on. I was lucky and chose the right business. Now this project gives me a chance to provide a useful way of life for my brother and others like him with similar problems.'

'Can I assume that this indicates you have just the slightest hint of a soft centre?' she asked wryly and was sure she saw him blush.

* * *

Sam spent a restless night. She was worried by the thought of the role Jackson was expecting of her. Maybe fate does control our destinies, she thought, and now it had driven her to this place and to Jackson.

Her alarm said six o'clock. She rolled over and closed her eyes again but it was much too late for satisfactory sleep. She might as well get up and make an early start. There was plenty to do, for heaven's sake.

She pottered around tidying and getting things ready for breakfast. Several cups of coffee later, she was feeling ready to tackle the day.

They had agreed to give Jackson their answers today. For her, she knew there was no real decision to be made. She couldn't possibly turn down his offer, giving up on the project that had come to mean so much.

'Why are you crashing round at this hour?' Allie grumbled when she appeared in the kitchen.

'I'm hardly crashing. But I couldn't sleep and it seemed like a good idea to get an early start. Now, how about a cooked breakfast?'

'No thanks. Toast as usual, please. I'll get my shower first though. I hope these early mornings aren't going to become a habit. I need my beauty sleep.'

Sam smiled as her daughter staggered through to the bathroom.

Later, as they waited at the bus stop, they saw Will coming out of the lodge. He waved and walked towards them.

'He hasn't got Jenny with him,' moaned Allie. 'Where's Jenny?' she called out to him.

'Sleeping off a restless night. I could hear the pups rampaging round half the night,' he called back. 'You just wait till Millie moves in with you. You'll understand. No more peace for you, my girl.'

'When can I have her?' she asked.

'Next week sometime. They're nearly ready to leave their mother.'

'Have you found homes for them all?' Sam asked.

'Most of them. I may keep one of them myself. Depends on what happens.' He looked at Sam meaningfully but she made no comment as the school bus arrived.

'Bye,' Allie called, clambering aboard. She sat next to one of her friends and didn't even notice the two adults as they waved her off.

'She seems to have settled down well,' Will remarked and Sam nodded. 'Look, can you spare a few minutes?' he asked. 'I want to chat through Jackson's bombshells of yesterday. I'm not sure what to think.'

They walked back to the lodge and went inside where Jenny and the puppies greeted them both like long-lost friends. Frowning, Will shut them in the porch, inviting Sam to sit in the warm kitchen. Without asking, he poured her some coffee from the filter machine.

'I want to tell you a bit more about myself.'

'I'll have to take a course in counselling,' Sam remarked, thinking, 'Jackson last night and now Will'.

'What do you mean?' he asked.

She shook her head. 'Nothing. Go on.'

'You've probably gathered that I was a teacher,' he said and Sam nodded. 'Well, I worked in a residential home for people with learning difficulties. The same one that Jackson's brother lives in. You do know Jackson has a brother, I suppose?'

'He's told me about him.'

'Dominic's a difficult bloke to be with, but harmless. Just rather heavy-going for twenty-four hours a day. Well, to cut a long story short, there was some trouble with one of the women residents. She developed a crush on me and then accused me of having an affair with her. It was all quite ridiculous. I was married and we'd just had a baby. Naturally my wife was upset. To make matters worse, she — my wife — was suffering severe post natal depression at the time and she wasn't coping. The accusation was the final straw. She was distraught.'

Sam could see that he was very upset. 'You don't have to talk about this, if you don't want to,' she whispered.

'I want you to know the whole story — ' He was interrupted by the ringing of the telephone. The answering machine cut in and Jackson's voice filled the room.

'Where are you, Will?' he demanded.

'I was expecting your decision by nine this morning. Come to my office A.S.A.P., please.'

'Darn it,' Will snapped. 'I s'pose we'll have to do this later.'

'We'd better go,' she agreed. 'It doesn't make any difference to your decision, does it?'

'Maybe not. But it might make a difference to the future,' he added. His look suggested that he had a great deal more to say.

Together, they left the lodge and walked over to the house.

'I'll leave you to it,' Sam decided. 'I'm going to look at something. P'raps you'd tell Jackson I'll be in the office in an hour or so?'

He gave a shrug and nodded. 'OK. I'll see you later. Could we have dinner this evening? Somewhere posh maybe? Then you can wear one of those posh outfits that Allie keeps telling me about.'

'I'm not sure it's a good idea.'

'Please,' he begged. 'It's the only way

I'll have time to tell you everything.'

'OK,' Sam replied doubtfully.

★　★　★

'How did your meeting with Will go?' she asked Jackson when she returned to the office.

'He's accepted, of course. Have you reached your decision?'

'How could I turn it down? It's the answer to my dream, isn't it?'

'Great. My legal chaps are sorting out contracts. Looks like it's all happening, doesn't it, Mrs Rayner?'

'I guess so.'

'Right. I must start clearing my desk,' he said.

'Clear your desk?' she echoed. 'Whatever for?'

'Helen starts on Monday — the new secretary. We're moving into the new offices. They're coming first thing to lay cables and do the necessary work. The office furniture is coming later today. You can go and help install it where you want it. I'll see to my own office.'

'But which *is* your office?'

'The one with the large desk. See you later.'

Sam gritted her teeth. That certainly told her where she stood. He'd organised everything. And there was a new secretary to cope with.

★ ★ ★

The 'posh' dinner with Will was at a pleasant restaurant inland from the coast. Sam felt relaxed, though she hadn't forgotten the prospect of his revelations. When the coffee arrived, Will's moment also arrived.

'Sam, I think you know what I'm going to say,' he began.

'About your wife? That she reacted badly to the accusations.'

'That wasn't quite what I meant, but I s'pose we'd better get it out of the way. The trouble is, once someone has been accused of improper conduct, it's very hard to lose the sticky mud. Even when I was proved completely innocent, I was aware that people were staring. My poor, sick wife couldn't cope and packed herself and the baby into the car and drove away.'

'Oh, Will, how terrible! What happened?' she asked.

He stared out of the dark window, his eyes moist.

'She was in a bad way. Very severe post-natal depression, as I said. She crashed the car and they were both killed. I left the school as soon as I could. The case came to nothing, but the local newspapers got hold of the story. Innocent or guilty, it didn't matter. It made good headlines.'

'Oh, Will, I'm so sorry,' Sam mumbled.

No wonder he was so cagey about himself and his past. It also explained why Jackson knew of Will's past, and also why Jackson was constantly warning her off.

'Let's leave,' Will suggested. 'Finish our talk somewhere private.'

He drove in the opposite direction from Pengelly Hall, stopping high on the cliffs overlooking the spectacular neighbouring bay. The lights of the nearby town flickered and the full moon was reflected across the waves.

'It's lovely here,' Sam breathed.

'It's a favourite haunt of mine. I come here to think. I want to finish telling you my story.'

'Not if it upsets you to talk about it.'

'It is upsetting, but I have to do it if there is to be any future for us.'

Sam felt herself growing tense. 'Will, I . . .'

'No, Sam, hear me out. I suppose I'd become too involved with the job. Committees and so on. So much that my wife couldn't believe I was out innocently for so many evenings. When the stupid accusations were made, Marie was ready to believe the worst of me. She wasn't stable, you realise. We had a blazing row. After Marie and the baby were gone, I was in a dreadful state. I felt responsible for the accident

. . . her depression, everything. It was as though I was being punished. I came back home here to Pengelly. I didn't want anything more to do with education.

'When I came back here, it seemed so safe and comfortable. And now I'm ready to make a commitment again, if you'll have me. What do you say, Sam? Will you marry me? I love you, and I love Allie too.'

'Oh, Will. You're very important to me. And Allie adores you, but I can't. Marriage . . . well, I'm not sure it's possible.'

'I love you, Sam. I need you. Please,' he added desperately, 'don't reject me.'

Sam's eyes filled with tears. She didn't want to hurt this man who was so dear to her. But marry him? She'd failed in one marriage and was so afraid to risk it again.

'I'm sorry, Will.'

He reached out and pulled her to him, pressing his lips against hers.

'Please,' she murmured. 'I can't do it,

Will. I'm so sorry. I don't think I can love you the way you deserve.'

'You're hoping Jackson will ask you . . . but you haven't a hope.'

'Will, it isn't like that!' she protested. 'There's nothing between me and Jackson.'

'I find that hard to believe. I'll take you home,' he said icily.

He drove home. They exchanged not a single word.

Two Men, One Heart

She kept herself frantically busy for the next few days. She and Jackson had a short meeting each day to outline plans and strategies. Helen, the new secretary, was given her tasks for the day. Sam saw nothing of Will. She hoped that her refusal hadn't ruined their relationship.

Allie was becoming anxious about her new puppy.

'You go and sort it out yourself,' Sam told her firmly. 'Ask Will to tell you exactly what you need and we'll go and buy the things after school. Then Millie can move in with us.'

'Yes!' Allie said, triumphantly punching the air. She scampered off to the lodge, hoping Will would be there, but she returned a few minutes later looking disappointed.

'He's probably busy somewhere,'

Sam tried to comfort her.

'The Land-Rover's gone and there's no sign of Jenny or the puppies in their run.'

Will had built an outdoor run for the dogs. They were usually out for most of the afternoons and it was Allie's favourite place after school.

'He's probably left them inside in case he's late back.'

All evening, Allie kept looking to see if there were any lights at Will's.

'Do you think we should go over?' she asked anxiously. 'It's not like him to be away for this long. Jenny and the puppies could be starving to death.'

'Of course they won't, silly. He'll have left food and water. Ring him if you want.'

Allie rang his number but got the answering machine.

'Can I go and see? To make sure the dogs are all right?'

The truth was, Sam was becoming a little anxious herself.

'You get ready for bed,' she said at

last. 'I'll go and see if everything's OK. Mrs Roberts is next door so you'll be fine for a few minutes, won't you?'

Allie nodded and Sam went out into the night.

Will's house was in darkness and the Land-Rover was missing. She could hear the dogs moving around in the little porch. Jenny barked and she could hear little puppy yips. Of Will there was no sign.

At the Hall, the lights were on in the old office, so she pushed the door open and found Jackson working at the computer.

'I just wondered if Will's here, but I see he isn't. He's out somewhere and the dogs are shut in. Allie's worried.'

'I'll go and check that he's back later. Why not stay for a drink?'

'Allie's on her own.'

'As you wish,' Jackson replied. 'Good night then.'

Sam felt a sense of foreboding. There was something unpleasant brewing but there was little she could do.

She went to bed early, but had just settled down when she heard noises outside. Shouting. It sounded like Will, and the second voice must be Jackson.

'Don't be such a fool, Will. Stop it.'

Will began to shout back. His voice was thick and distorted. He had obviously been drinking. 'You rat! You think you can buy everyone, don't you? But you hurt her and you'll have me to deal with.'

There was more shouting and then crashing sounds. Sam flung some clothes on and rushed outside.

'Will? Jackson? What on earth's going on?' She could see two dark shapes rolling on the ground. 'Stop it! Stop it!' she yelled. 'What are you doing, Will? You're drunk.'

She tried to intervene and ended up being thrown to the ground herself. As she squealed, it was like cold water hitting the men. They fell apart and leapt to see what was wrong.

'Sam, Sam, are you all right?' Will shouted. 'I'm so sorry, Sam.'

'Idiot! Imbecile!' yelled Jackson, along with a few more expletives.

'I'm all right.' She stood up, feeling slightly dazed.

'I think it's time you left,' said Jackson stonily to Will. 'Go home. I'll see you first thing in the morning.'

Will was still muttering under his breath as he wove across the lawn.

'Let's get inside,' Jackson urged. 'We're both cold and wet and shaken.' He brushed at the mud on his clothes and led Sam towards the main door.

'I left my door open,' she said shakily. 'I'll go that way.'

'I'll put some coffee on. And we both need a brandy,' Jackson insisted. 'Make sure Allie's OK and come through.'

She looked in on Allie, who was still sleeping peacefully, then stood under a hot shower and began to feel warm again. She dried herself and pulled on a clean t-shirt and jeans.

'What on earth was going on?' she asked as soon as she was in Jackson's kitchen.

'He was banging at my door, yelling. Threw a punch at me as soon as he saw me. I've no idea what brought it on.'

'I do. He asked me to marry him and I turned him down. He thinks it's all your fault. But he never drinks much. Not normally.'

He gazed at her. 'My fault? So you've got two men fighting over you?'

'Come off it, Jackson. You weren't fighting over me. Will had just had too much to drink and couldn't handle it.'

'Anyone who can get in that state has no right to be working with young people. As of tomorrow, he's looking for another job.'

'You're firing him? But you can't!'

'Just watch me.'

'But what about your plans? He's essential.'

'I can find a dozen folk who could do the job. They'll be queuing up.'

She was anxious about the effect it would have on Allie if Will was suddenly to disappear from her life. She had to persuade Jackson to relent.

'What happened?' she ventured when she found Jackson in his office the next morning.

'What do you think? I gave him a month's notice to quit the lodge. He let me down. I owe Will Heston nothing. I had already kept him on here against my better judgement.'

'But he's worked so hard!' Sam protested. 'All those months. You can't send him packing after one small incident.'

'Small incident? I could take out charges of common assault.'

Feeling responsible, she turned and walked away. Will was such a good friend, she would miss him badly if he left the area. And Allie would be devastated.

She needed an excuse to go and see Will. She could ask about Allie's puppy and what she needed to buy.

The dogs barked their welcome from the confines of their little run. When

Will opened the door she gazed at him in horror. He was unshaven, hair tousled and he was clearly nursing a dreadful hangover.

'What do you want?' he demanded.

'I came to say I'm sorry. Will, you look awful. I'll make you some coffee.'

She put two slices of dry toast beside him and a mug of coffee and ordered him to eat, but he'd fallen asleep. She checked that Jenny and the puppies had food and water and left, feeling unbelievably sad.

She made several trips to the lodge during the day but Will remained in the same position on the sofa. Somehow she had to break the news of his imminent departure to Allie. And she hated the thought of him being absent from this project they had begun together.

★ ★ ★

The work progressed and she was kept busy but Will was giving her great concern. No doubt Jackson was looking for a replacement but it would take time for a new person to get up to speed. She sighed. Later on she must go over to see Will and try to discover his plans, if he had made any. Dear Will. How she was going to miss him.

She was saved the trouble when he arrived at her apartment.

'Will. I haven't seen you for days. How are you? Come in.'

'Thanks. I wanted to talk, if it's convenient.'

'Of course. Me too.'

'I'm so sorry. I've really screwed everything up, haven't I? I've missed you.'

Sam felt tears spring to her eyes. She'd missed him too.

'Are you all right? You haven't been drinking again?'

'No, don't worry. I'll never make that mistake again. I haven't touched a drop since that dreadful night. But time is so short. Do you realise that I have to vacate my home next week? And I've nowhere to go. That place is all I've known since I came back to Cornwall. I love it and love my job. Yet one stupid mistake and the whole lot's ruined.'

'It was a pretty mega mistake,' she commented ruefully. 'Of all the people to choose, Jackson was probably the worst.'

'I know. But I'm begging you — will you think again about us? Give me another chance?'

'I'll think about it,' Sam promised. 'And I'll see if I can persuade Jackson to extend your tenancy.'

'Thank you.' He looked at her with such undisguised longing that she put her hands out to him and drew him into a hug. He dropped a light kiss on to her cheek and left.

'I hope you make it up with Will. And get his job back. He's been so unhappy,' said Allie from her bedroom door.

'Were you listening?' Sam accused.

'I couldn't help it. Will's so nice, Mum. Much nicer than Jackson. I know he's very, very rich but he can be very mean.'

'What do you mean?' asked Sam in surprise.

'He tells me I'm a nuisance and in the way.' Allie looked at her feet, ill at ease. 'Oh, Mum, are you going to marry him instead of Will? At first I thought it might be a good idea, but not if it makes everything different.'

'I'm not planning to marry anyone. You don't understand, Allie. This is grown-up stuff.'

'I s'pose,' she said grudgingly. 'But you must admit, it does affect me too. 'Night.' She went back into her room and shut the door.

* * *

The next morning, Sam set out to tackle her boss. 'Jackson, I need to talk about Will. He hasn't got anywhere else to go . . .'

'That's his problem.'

'I know, but I need him. I can't do everything myself. He understands what needs doing. We planned everything together. I need someone now.'

'Very eloquent. You rehearsed your speech well.'

'For heaven's sake, Jackson, the entire world doesn't run on clockwork. People have feelings. Needs.'

'Oh, do whatever you think best. I haven't time for all this emotional stuff. But if he does one single thing even an inch out of line, you're both out.'

She smiled with relief. 'Thanks, Jackson. You won't regret it, I'm sure.'

'I'd better not. I have to go away now but we'll have dinner on Friday.'

'But Phil's coming down on Friday.'

'He'd better come as well then.'

'I'll tell him. Thanks. Have a good trip.'

Will was very impressed with her powers of persuasion when she went to the lodge to tell him the good news.

'You are one wonderful lady! Don't worry, I've learned my lesson.'

The puppies and Jenny were gambolling around their feet and Sam laughed. 'Careful. Allie would never forgive us if we squashed her beloved Millie!'

'Talking of which, she's ready to leave her mum.'

'Tomorrow,' Sam promised. 'There's too much to do now. Get to work, man, there's planting to be organised.'

This was the best part. After all the clearing, planning and ordering, the plants were finally going into the ground.

When she told Allie that her puppy could come and join them the next day, the girl squealed with excitement and they went straight out to buy everything they'd need . . . collar and lead, puppy food and several toys. Sam also picked up carpet stain remover and air freshener.

'Just in case!' Sam told Allie.

By the time Jackson returned at the weekend, things were moving fast. In great excitement, Sam told him of the progress.

'Do you want to come and see what we've done?' she asked enthusiastically but he shook his head. He seemed distracted.

'Dinner at seven-thirty,' he told her.

By seven-thirty, there was no sign of Phil, but Jackson came through with a bottle of champagne.

'I thought you might like a drink while we wait.'

'Do you really like that stuff?' Allie asked curiously. 'Or do you just drink it because you can afford it?'

'Allie! Don't be rude!' Sam said quickly.

'Well, I think it's very over-rated,' the girl said sulkily and plonked herself down in front of the television. Jackson scowled.

'Turn it down, Allie,' Sam ordered. 'In fact, you can turn it off.'

'But I always watch this! It's not fair. I thought you were going out.'

'We're waiting for Uncle Phil.'

'Go without him. At least *he's* pleased to have me around.'

'Allie, that's enough. Go to your room. Now!'

Grumpily, she slouched from the room.

'You should send her to boarding-school,' said Jackson with a scowl. 'Free your time. I'll put you in touch with a couple of good schools. And I'll help with the fees.'

'How can you even think of that?' she protested. 'I would never send her away.'

Allie, still within earshot, burst into the room, near to tears. 'Mummy, you can't send me away! Please don't, Mummy. I don't want to go away.'

'You'll do what your mother tells you, young lady,' Jackson returned coldly. 'Any decisions made are for your own good. Now, I believe you were told to go to your room. Your mother and I have things to discuss. And don't let me find that you have been listening at doors again.'

Allie paled and Sam could see her eyes filling with tears. Silently the girl turned and went into her bedroom, but before Sam could voice her anger to Jackson about speaking to her daughter like that the doorbell rang and Phil breezed in. 'Hi there, sis. How're things?'

'You must have heard the cork pop,' Jackson said, suddenly full of bonhomie as he filled three glasses.

'Now this is what I call a welcome,' Phil approved. 'But where's my best girl? Don't tell me she's started dating already?'

'She's in her room,' Sam said quietly, and flashed a warning at him with her eyes not to pursue the matter right now.

Thanks to Phil, the evening was pleasant enough.

'I gather your sister's got the diggers booked for next month. Digging out ponds or something.' Jackson laughed. 'I've never known a woman who likes playing with mud quite so much.'

'She was always a tomboy,' Phil said with a curious look at his sister. Something wasn't right. She was too quiet.

'So, what's been going on? I sense an atmosphere,' Phil said when they were finally alone. 'Everything in the garden isn't quite as lovely, I gather.'

'Oh, Phil, I'm so confused,' Sam burst out at once. 'Will and Jackson had a fight and Will was sacked. Will asked me to marry him and I turned him down. Now Jackson's suggesting I should send Allie to boarding school, just so I can be at his beck and call, I'm sure. And you should have heard the way he spoke to her just now. He's lucky I didn't punch his lights out!'

'Wow!' It was a lot to take in. 'But how can you manage without Will?'

'I don't have to. I persuaded Jackson to take him back. I even promised Will I'd think again about his proposal.'

'You don't do things by halves, do you? Look, we'll talk tomorrow after you've had a decent sleep. Right now you look worn out — with good reason, by all accounts.'

★   ★   ★

After Phil's visit, Jackson reached an unexpected decision. 'I'm going away

306

for a while. This isn't really my scene. I'm going back to London to do what I do best. Phil will take care of everything I was planning to do. Send me regular reports. Twice a week should suffice.'

'Jackson . . . I . . . I'm very grateful for everything you've done. And I'll make you proud of the garden. The Gardens of Pengelly will be famous.'

'You bet they will.' With a smile he strode off.

'Goodbye, Jackson,' Sam whispered after him. She hoped this wasn't a sign that his interest in the project might be over.

She was anxious to oversee the re-creation of the jungle garden. The work was absorbing, but major problems began at once. Two days of constant downpour had turned the site into a quagmire and the diggers got stuck in a mud slide.

'It's pointless trying to work on this until the spring,' Will advised. 'I know how eager you are but it isn't feasible. I think we should move back to work on the walled gardens.'

'You're right,' Sam agreed sadly. 'Can you start organising it? I want to spend some time researching.'

She visited every church in the locality and made copious notes from the gravestones and poured over parish records. Finally, she wrote off for copies of a couple of birth certificates and a marriage certificate.

It took several days for her to get any replies. A boy child had been registered as Henry Heston in September 1916. The mother's maiden name was recorded as Victoria Cobb. Though the evidence suggested otherwise, Sam remained convinced that this child was Will's own grandfather. With the war raging round Europe, deaths and births had been frequent and records may have been kept less than accurately.

Mrs Roberts remembered hearing about some scandal regarding the youngest daughter of the Westcotts. The girl had been sent away during the First World War. It was, of course, many years before her own time.

'I see what you're getting at,' Mrs Roberts said suddenly. 'The Heston boy might have been . . . the baby. It makes sense. There were rumours of a windfall in the Heston family.' She looked thoughtful.

'There was another scandal when Rosalie Westcott's daughter wanted to marry Henry Heston. Family was up in arms about it. Some nonsense about class. But if he was the son of the younger daughter, they'd have been closely related, wouldn't they?

'So, you think our own Will Heston could be the grandson of Marguerite Westcott?' she went on wonderingly. 'I suppose you found out about it in one of those books you read. They think it's all been hushed up and yet, someday, it all comes out.' Mrs Roberts smiled. 'And is the future going to bring a Heston to live here? I know he's sweet on you. And that dear little lass of yours. 'Bout time he had a bit of happiness.'

Sam grimaced. 'I think I've made too much of a mess of things for that.'

'He's a good man,' Mrs Roberts said with feeling. She had always had a soft spot for Will.

'I know,' Sam said regretfully. 'Please don't mention any of this to him, will you? Not yet. I'm waiting for some documents which will give me the final proof.'

Will didn't ask her to go out with him again and never once spoke of his feelings for her. Instead of brooding, she threw herself into work and the restoration progressed. The old greenhouses were demolished and the bricks carefully saved. New panels were being made by a team of carpenters, recruited from the surrounding villages.

At the beginning of December, Phil and his family moved down to Cornwall. They had bought a house in a village a couple of miles away. Allie's two boy cousins were taken in hand and shown round the Pengelly gardens and fully instructed on how to behave when they started their new school. They were to attend the last week of term so that they could get to know a few of the other children during the fun time that led up to Christmas.

'We ought to have a big family party at Christmas,' Allie suggested. 'Invite everyone we know. Lucinda, Mrs Roberts, Will. What do you think? We could use the dining-room in Jackson's apartment. He can come too, I s'pose.'

'It's his house. I guess he should be asked first of all,' Sam mused.

'Mrs Roberts says it's OK. I already asked her.'

'Oh, Allie, you're impossible!' But she promised to mention it to Jackson when she next spoke to him.

When Allie was in bed, she took out the red diary that had been an inspiration for so long. She knew it was the right time to share her secret. She dialled Will's number.

'Can you come over? I want to show you something.'

It was their first meeting alone for several weeks.

'I thought you might like to read this. I've had it for a while but I think now's the time to share it with you.' She handed him the diary that might have been written by his great-grandmother.

'Why give it to me? It's just the diary of a young girl. Long dead, no doubt.'

'There's information about the garden as it used to be. And other stuff as well. I'd like you to read it, Will. Take your time.'

He shrugged. 'Ok.'

They drank coffee, chatting spasmodically. Just occasionally Will looked relaxed enough to be his old self. It felt good.

'Look, I think I'd better go now,' he said abruptly. 'I'll read your book as soon as I can, but it doesn't sound like my sort of thing.'

She stood and went to the door with him where he brushed against her arm and went out into the night. No goodnight peck on the cheek.

★　★　★

'This is going to be the best Christmas ever,' Allie said happily after a bout of serious shopping. She had gone off on her own to buy a present for Sam, and there was much giggling and calls of 'no peeping' as the heaps of bright carriers were stowed in the back of the van.

Jackson had given his blessing to the Christmas party in the old library and Mrs Roberts was working to fill the larder with Christmas goodies.

'I've been waiting for an occasion like this for years,' she said happily. 'Ever since the second Miss Marguerite left nearly forty years since.'

'The second Marguerite?' echoed Sam.

'Yes. The last surviving Westcott, I believe. She'd been living with some relative, I think. Poor old thing must be all alone now.'

'Why didn't you mention her before? How old is she?' Sam asked excitedly. Surely she couldn't possibly be the same Marguerite? She'd be over a hundred if it was *her* Marguerite.

'I reckon she must be eighty at least.

She was Miss Rosalie's daughter.'

'Of course,' Sam breathed. Will's aunt. Probably his only real living relative. 'Do you have her address? We could ask her to come for Christmas.' She could hardly believe Mrs Roberts had never mentioned her.

'I doubt she'd want to come back here. But yes, I do have an address. I don't know why you'd want to bother though.'

Sam quickly typed a letter. It seemed to make the circle complete.

When there was no reply, she assumed the old lady was too infirm to travel, or maybe she had died. However, the day before Christmas Eve, she received a call. Miss Marguerite Westcott would be pleased to accept her invitation to stay for Christmas. She apologised for the late acceptance but she had been away from home for several weeks.

Sam hugged the information to herself, planning to arrange a meeting between Will and his aunt as soon as she arrived the following day. She had another urgent matter to discuss with Will, too. She suddenly knew in her heart that she was ready to make a commitment.

He was standing in the Italian garden. He was wearing muddy jeans, boots and the inevitable comfy old sweater. But he was Will. The man that, at last, she knew she truly loved.

'Will? Can you spare me a few minutes?' she said breathlessly. 'There's something I want to say. A few weeks ago you asked me to marry you. I turned you down. But I've sorted myself out since then. I was frightened of being hurt again, but I know now that all my worries were foolish. I'm truly free now, in my heart and my mind. I love you, Will Heston. Will you marry me?'

For a moment he stared at her, then he grabbed her round the waist, lifted her off her feet and whirled her round, yelling at the top of his voice, 'Yes! Yes! Yes!'

Suddenly they both stumbled to the ground, a tangle of arms and legs.

'What on earth did you fall over?' Sam asked, giggling.

'I don't know. A rock. A stone. A fallen tree stump. Who cares?'

Sam pulled away the yard of ivy and vegetation — and found the thing she had been looking for for so long. The old sundial.

'Now that is something,' she murmured. 'Quite a significant find at such a moment, don't you think?'

'Shut up, woman, and come here.' He drew her into his arms and kissed her with a thoroughness that she thought would never end.

They were finally roused by the sound of a round of applause, and found a bunch of workmen had formed a grinning circle round them.

Sam blushed violently. 'Go away! We're busy planning the next phase.' She turned to Will. 'Here, help me pull this sundial up. You know, I think it's more or less intact.'

'The metal arm's bent. It's at least three hours fast,' Will said seriously.

'We couldn't have found it at a more perfect moment.'

'Sam, I read your book. I don't see why you kept so quiet about it. It would have helped during the planning.'

'I always made sure I told you everything you needed to know. But much more importantly, it's the people. Haven't you realised? I'm certain Marguerite was your great-grandmother. Henry Cobb was your great-grandfather. Their child was adopted by the Heston family and he became your grandfather.'

'Sounds too confusing to a simple soul like me. Can you prove it?'

Sam nodded. She now had the written proof.

'So I'm descended from the Westcott family? The owners of all this at one time?' he said wonderingly. 'Ironic, me being back here as a gardener.'

'Head Gardener, no less. Much higher up than your great-grandfather.'

She smiled. 'I'd like to keep our plans a secret, if that's all right with you. Until Christmas Day.'

'The men won't say anything. We'll tell the family at Christmas dinner. Allie will be OK about it, won't she?'

'Ecstatic,' Sam said with absolute certainty.

The next morning, Sam drove to the station to collect Marguerite Westcott, a charming lady in her eighties.

'I understand you're doing wonderful things to the garden, my dear,' she said in her cultured tones. 'I'm so looking forward to seeing it. It was in a dreadful state by the time I left. You have a huge task ahead of you.'

They chatted easily, the common bond of this magical place bringing them together. Sam showed her the photographs she had kept so carefully. Marguerite knew most of the people.

When she came to the picture of the sundial, she stopped and stared. 'Why, you even have a picture of me!'

'You? That's amazing. You see, we

discovered the sundial only yesterday. We must take another picture of you while you're here. In the same spot, if we can drag you through the under-growth!'

Will came into the office. 'Oh, I'm sorry, I didn't realise you were with someone. I'll come back later.'

'No, Will. I want you to meet Marguerite Westcott — niece of your great-grandmother.'

The expression on Will's face was a mixture of surprise and wonder.

'Marguerite, this is Will Heston. He really is the great-grandson of your Aunt Marguerite and Henry Cobb, the gardener she loved so much.'

'You have her eyes,' the old lady said softly. 'She was a charming woman. I only got to know her in her final years, when I came back here to be with her. She was quite a beauty in her day. The family never got over the scandal she caused. She never married, of course. Lived the life of a recluse for years. At least she was with someone from the

319

family for her last years. I was named for her, so it seemed the correct thing to do. Will, my dear, I am so thrilled to meet you.'

★　★　★

However much they all tried to help, Mrs Roberts remained in full charge of the Christmas lunch, though Lucinda Jones was graciously allowed into the kitchen just before the meal was served.

Half an hour before they were to sit down at the table, Jackson arrived, clutching a couple of magnums of champagne. 'Hope you don't mind but it seemed foolish to spend Christmas alone and I knew Mrs Roberts would have masses of food.'

Sam glanced at Will, who gave her a wink. Nothing was going to spoil his day and the announcement he planned to make.

Jackson poured champagne for everyone and handed the glasses round, quickly assuming the role of host. It was his house, after all.

'A toast,' he called. 'To Pengelly, past and present.' They all joined in raising their glasses. 'You'd better introduce me,' he said quietly to Sam.

'In a minute,' she replied. 'Listen, everyone — we have an announcement.' Everyone smiled and nodded. 'We're getting married,' she announced.

'Who's 'we'?' asked Jeremy, the younger of Phil's sons.

'Mum and Jackson, of course,' said Allie, looking miserable.

'No, we're not. It's Will and I who are getting married.'

'Will? Thank heavens for that!' Allie said more cheerfully.

Sam turned to Jackson. He was smiling, along with everyone else.

'Congratulations. I'm sure you're going to be very happy. Now, let's drink a toast and then maybe we can eat. I'm starving.'

After the enormous Christmas dinner Mrs Roberts had laid on, they all went into the main hall to open the presents under the tree.

Shyly Sam held out a package to Marguerite. 'I think you should have this,' she murmured softly.

The old lady lifted her eyes and looked into Sam's. 'Why, thank you, my dear, but you shouldn't be giving me gifts as well as your wonderful hospitality. What you are doing is all the reward I could ever want.'

She pulled away the gold paper and revealed the slim red leather book that had become so much a part of Sam's life. She fingered the cover and opened the first page. Her eyes filled with tears.

'Thank you, Sam. Thank you so much.'

When she had finished talking to his aunt, Will drew Sam to one side and gave her a small package. 'No guesses as to what this is,' he said softly.

The jewel box held an antique ring, an emerald set in a circle of diamonds and mounted on a gold band.

'Oh, Will. It's beautiful! But it must

have cost a fortune.'

'Probably did once. You have Marguerite to thank for this. It belonged to her own great-grandmother. It should have been given to our Marguerite but she missed out because of her scandalous behaviour. It did seem appropriate, in the circumstances.'

'You know, Will, I do believe there is a bit of the old romantic in you after all! I do so love you, and I'm sorry I took so long to decide.'

And with that they kissed, while Allie watched and nodded with a look of extreme satisfaction. About time too!

The End.

We do hope that you have enjoyed reading this large print book.

Did you know that all of our titles are available for purchase?

We publish a wide range of high quality large print books including:
Romances, Mysteries, Classics
General Fiction
Non Fiction and Westerns

Special interest titles available in large print are:
The Little Oxford Dictionary
Music Book, Song Book
Hymn Book, Service Book

Also available from us courtesy of Oxford University Press:
Young Readers' Dictionary
(large print edition)
Young Readers' Thesaurus
(large print edition)

For further information or a free brochure, please contact us at:
Ulverscroft Large Print Books Ltd.,
The Green, Bradgate Road, Anstey,
Leicester, LE7 7FU, England.
Tel: (00 44) **0116 236 4325**
Fax: (00 44) **0116 234 0205**

LOVE'S DAWNING

Diney Delancey

Rosanne Charlton joins her friend Ruth and family for a holiday in Southern Ireland. Unfortunately, the holiday is marred for her by the arrival of Ruth's brother, Brendan O'Neill, whom Rosanne has always disliked. However, Brendan's presence is not Rosanne's only problem . . . Trouble and danger close round her, like an Irish mist, when she becomes unwittingly involved in mysterious activities in the bay — and finds herself fighting for survival in the dark waters of the Atlantic.

BETRAYAL OF INNOCENCE

Valerie Holmes

Annie works hard to keep her father from the poorhouse. However, she is wracked with guilt as she watches her friend, Georgette Davey, being used by Lady Constance. Annie longs to escape her life at the Hall, taking Georgette with her — but how? The arrival of the mysterious doctor, Samuel Speer, adds to her dilemma as Annie's concern for her friend grows. Georgette's innocence has been betrayed, but Annie is unaware of the threat that hangs over her own.

THE RELUCTANT BRIDE

Dorothy Purdy

Christine is forced into marriage with Adam Kyle, a wealthy and handsome entrepreneur whom she despises, in order to save her late father's reputation. At first Christine wants nothing to do with him; she tells him she hates everything he stands for. But during their honeymoon in the Friendly Islands her opinion of him changes, and she realises that she has misjudged him. Now she no longer feels embittered, true love blossoms among the sheltering palms.

SUSPICIOUS HEART

Joyce Johnson

Chantelle Wilde is a research interviewer for a film company, driving to Villefleurs in the South of France to interview the film star Heloise Remondin. But after she is hit by another car, the handsome driver, Phillipe Blanchard, insists on helping her to repair the damage. When she arrives at Madame Remondin's, she's surprised to discover that he is her grandson. Although she'd vowed never to love again, she hadn't reckoned with the arrogant Phillipe Blanchard.

DARK GUARDIAN

Rebecca King

When Fliss Naughton found herself stranded on a desert island with the mysterious Brand Carradine, she was at a loss as to what to do. He was her captor, but he was also her legal guardian — and she was at his mercy. Why then, as the time came for her to leave, did she find it increasingly difficult parting from him? Could it be that she truly longed for nothing better than to be by his side?

ONLY ONE CAN PLAY

Mary Landy

Living in Barnscombe in Devon, Karen and Greg were happily married, but after a series of suspicious accidents, Karen left her husband. Who would want to harm her? Surely not Greg himself, or Mark, his partner? Or Tim, her first love, with his own life to lead? As for her sister, Jenny, men to her were just stepping-stones to success. Karen needed to leave Devon to find the answers — she might not live long enough if she stayed.